# MAKER

ISBN 978-1-77186-259-2 pbk; 978-1-77186-260-8 epub; 978-1-77186-261-5 pdf

Cover by Maison 1608
Book Design by Folio infographie
Editing and proofreading by Blossom Thom, Robin Philpot, Rachel Hewitt

Legal Deposit, 3rd quarter 2021
Bibliothèque et Archives nationales du Québec
Library and Archives Canada

Published by Baraka Books of Montreal

Printed and bound in Quebec

Trade Distribution & Returns
Canada – UTP Distribution: UTPdistribution.com

United States
Independent Publishers Group: IPGbook.com

We acknowledge the support from the Société de développement des entreprises culturelles (SODEC) and the Government of Quebec tax credit for book publishing administered by SODEC.

Société de développement des entreprises culturelles
Québec

Funded by the Government of Canada
Financé par le gouvernement du Canada | Canada

Jim Upton

# MAKER

## A Novel

Baraka
Books
Montréal

*For Tom, Kay, and Jeff,*
*and all those with whom I have had the pleasure*
*to collaborate in one capacity or another*

# Chapter 1

As Nicole was about to complete her fiftieth lap, a body in black surged by and bounced off the wall ahead of her. Twenty minutes later, she hoisted herself onto the edge of the pool and removed her cap and goggles. The endorphins were just kicking in when someone tapped her on the shoulder. She gazed up at a tall woman in a black bathing suit.

"Nicole Fortin? I thought it was you. I'm Elsie Bernier. We used to swim together in the club."

It took a moment to connect the dots. "Elsie. Of course." Nicole scrambled to her feet, and the two women hugged. "Were you swimming in my lane? That's why I couldn't keep up. The distance swimmers never had a chance against you sprinters."

Elsie grinned. "How many years has it been? We were still teenagers."

"It's been ages. Why haven't we run into each other before?"

"This is my first time here in years," Elsie said. "I just moved back to Montreal from Calgary with my husband and two kids. We live in Pointe-Claire, but I wanted to return for a swim in the old stomping grounds. Do any of the others from the club ever show up?"

"Not that I've noticed."

Elsie swept the hair from her forehead. "You know who I ran into last week? Gabriel Nadeau. He's working with my son's swim team on the West Island. I had such a crush on him when he was coaching us."

At the mention of his name, Nicole's mouth opened, but no words came. They picked up their towels and walked towards the locker room.

"So, tell me about yourself," Elsie said.

"I live with my daughter, Julie. She's just started university and reminds me of myself at her age, though she's made better choices than I did."

As they dressed, Nicole tried to steer the conversation back onto Elsie, who suggested they exchange phone numbers before parting ways.

Nicole plodded back to the parking lot behind the sports complex on Émile-Journault Avenue, reeling from the encounter. Her past had sideswiped her present, and she was caught up in the wreckage.

Once inside her car, she buckled up and stared through the windshield. In place of the overcast sky, she saw her mother jumping up and down in the stands of the Olympic pool on Pierre-De Coubertin Avenue, fists clenched and arms pumping, as Shannon Smith nipped the New Zealand swimmer at the wall for the bronze medal in 1976. Nicole could describe the scene in precise detail, even though she never witnessed the event itself. Earlier that day, she'd been offloaded to her *mamie* and was kneeling on a kitchen chair pouring milk into a bowl of sugar and flour, unaware her life was about to change.

Not long after, she took her first swimming lesson. Two years later, she was guided into a local club, and by her eighteenth birthday, was ranked second nationally in the 400 metre freestyle. Her mother kept a scrapbook documenting Nicole's swimming career. It even included clippings from the English-language press. She told her daughter that becoming the next Canadian woman to win an Olympic medal at this distance would be "a closing of the circle." That goal became their shared dream.

"We're going back to the source," her mother gushed, on learning the national swim trials for the 1992 Barcelona Games were scheduled for Montreal.

The morning of her race, Nicole had a light breakfast, then vomited. She figured that was a good sign. It meant she was jacked.

Raymond phoned and promised to steal away from his salesman's job at the car dealership in time to catch her swim. When she first mentioned they were seeing each other, her mother had stopped rinsing the dishes.

"But he's older than you and already working. What does that mean for your future?"

"Don't worry," Nicole assured her mother. "My grades are good, I'm applying to university, and I'll still be part of the swim club."

A few weeks later, he suggested she move in with him.

"It's just not possible, Ray. With my swimming and school, that's enough to juggle at the moment."

He leaned in and brushed his lips against hers. Nicole couldn't recall how their clothes ended up on the floor, but as she lay in his arms, there was no feeling of guilt, only a deep and drowsy restfulness.

The day of the Olympic trials, she sat in the back of her parent's car tingling with anticipation. As they drove across town, she closed her eyes and visualized the race. She usually trailed after the first few lengths before her strength and stamina hauled in taller rivals over the final laps. And that's the way the swim unfolded in her head.

The actual event played out differently. Nicole pushed herself to the end but struggled to maintain her focus and finished fourth. As she walked off the pool deck, Gabriel came over from where the coaches were gathered. He put an arm around her shoulders, and her body stiffened.

"Don't dwell on this," he said. "You're still young."

Nicole nodded but kept her eyes lowered until he released his grip and turned away to watch the next race.

She changed in a daze, then rejoined her parents and Raymond in the foyer. Her mother's face conveyed the hint of a smile, but it was forced and hard. She looked through Nicole and beyond. Her father stared blankly in disbelief. After the requisite hugs, Ray kissed her on the cheek and promised to call later. She trudged to the parking lot alongside her parents, tears streaming down her face. Her mother passed her a tissue.

Once they reached home, Nicole headed for her room and collapsed on the bed. As the highest-ranked member of her swim team, she had been expected to challenge for the national title and make the squad for Barcelona. Instead, she managed to plunge from promising Olympic hope to eighteen-year-old has-been.

Next morning, after her mother went to work at the tobacco factory in St. Henri and her father left for a small machine shop in LaSalle, Nicole skipped school and buried her head in a pillow.

Everything changed following her failure to qualify for the Barcelona Games. A few days later, her mother walked in on her as she was throwing up and asked how often this had happened. Within an hour, they were sitting in the neighbourhood health clinic when Nicole's name was called.

After the doctor examined her, he invited her mother to join them in the office and explained his findings. Her mother's face showed no emotion. She thanked him, rose from her chair, and walked silently from the room. Nicole followed, her eyes fixed on the floor.

"I blame myself for misjudging you," her mother said on the drive home. "I thought you were smarter than this."

Nicole blinked back tears. "We tried to be careful."

"Accidents can happen when you do things you shouldn't."

"There may still be time—"

Her mother's fist bounced off the steering wheel. "Don't even consider that! It's out of the question."

After returning from the clinic, Nicole phoned Raymond and arranged to meet him in a park nearby. They were seated on a wooden bench, gazing at the shimmering rapids of the St. Lawrence River in the distance. His eyes widened as she unburdened herself. When she finished, he put his arm around her and kissed the top of her head. "Wow, you and me parents," was all he said. They agreed to talk the next day.

That evening over dinner, Nicole avoided eye contact with her parents and concentrated on the glazed ham, green beans, and garlic-flavoured scalloped potatoes. Only the clink of cutlery on their ceramic plates broke the silence.

After her mother announced she was taking a bath, Nicole offered to clear the table and do the dishes. Then she ventured into the living room where her father was seated in a beige-cushioned glider reading the paper. His slippered feet were crossed at the ankles and resting on the ottoman.

"Dad, can I speak with you?"

He glanced up, before folding the paper and lowering it to his lap. "What is it you want?"

"I know I've hurt you and Mom, and I'm truly sorry for that. I'd do anything to change what's happened. I'm begging you not to freeze me out. Even if I don't deserve your support, I need it now more than ever."

He rose from the chair and squinted from behind his glasses. "You had a chance to make something of your life, and you blew it." His garlic-scented words splattered against her. "Have you forgotten all the sacrifices your mother's made, the early morning car rides to practice, the weekends out of town at competitions?"

Her knees wobbled, and a drop of sweat slid down her arm.

"And you repay her by getting knocked up."

He tossed the newspaper onto the chair and turned back to her. "The people your mother works with, her friends who have followed your swimming career, what does she tell them now? Can you imagine the shame she feels?"

The slap to her cheek was still smarting as she watched him walk away.

# Chapter 2

Two days after Nicole's chance encounter with Elsie at the pool, her mother called. "Your father and I booked a cruise out of Miami over Christmas to celebrate our fortieth wedding anniversary. We haven't seen you and Julie since August and won't be able to get together over the holidays because of our trip. Why don't the two of you come over for dinner next weekend? We'd appreciate a visit before our departure."

Nicole's parents had long ago given up on her but still harboured hopes for their granddaughter. A few times a year, they all shared a meal. On those rare occasions, Nicole tried to put the past aside. But the event was always an awkward affair. During their last visit, Julie happened to mention her success in registering for all the courses she wanted to take at school.

"That's good. You should grab your opportunities when they come along," her grandfather said, then stared at Nicole till she lowered her eyes.

Her parents had hidden their embarrassment at the wedding, joining with Raymond's family to wish them well. But they had never buried their disappointment with her. She wondered if that shared feeling was part of what held them together as a couple.

Rather than celebrating her marriage, Nicole had been relieved when the day was over. They rented the lower half of a duplex on Dollier Street, near Ray's workplace in Saint-Léonard. Though only a thirty-minute drive from her parents' home in Verdun, it seemed like another world. In place of the single-family, red brick houses dating from the Second World War, rows of modern units lined both sides of the street. An outing to nearby shops became a trip abroad, sprinkled with greetings of "Buongiorno" or "Ciao." And the listless air was no match for the breeze blowing off the St. Lawrence River, a couple of blocks from her parent's front door.

Nicole had graduated from CEGEP a month before the wedding, but instead of studying psychology at university found herself prepping for pregnancy and parenting. Having failed at her dream of winning an Olympic medal, she tried to compensate by being a model wife and mother.

When her ankles and feet began to swell, Raymond started calling her his "little elephant." That's not what Nicole needed to hear. Each time she spoke with her parents by phone, their conversations mirrored the chilly days of autumn. After Julie was born in December, Nicole's mother came by the hospital and remarked on the baby's resemblance to her daughter rather than Ray.

In the weeks that followed, Nicole's world oscillated between the daily chore of changing diapers and the mind-numbing routine of domestic duties. She was hard-wired for the faintest sound of crying at night and rose the next morning more exhausted than the previous day.

The stretch marks on her stomach illustrated how much her life had changed. She didn't even recognize her own body. Yet every time she nuzzled her infant daughter's head, there was a feeling of oneness she had never experienced with another human being.

Early on, she fended off Raymond with pleas of lingering pain. Later, she serviced his needs despite her own lack of interest. At least he was there for the baby and her, picking up what she needed at the drugstore, helping with the food shopping, and even doing his share of cleaning.

Four months after Julie's birth, he began going out on Thursday evenings for a game of poker with "the boys." One Friday morning, Nicole noticed a splotch of red on the pillow and glanced at Ray. The line of dried blood ran from a nostril to the top of his lip.

While he downed a coffee, she mentioned the blood. He dismissed it as just a nosebleed, but she caught the flash of panic in his eyes.

A few weeks later, he phoned to say working hours at the car dealership had been extended, and every salesman had to take a turn. He arrived home more energized than usual, despite the longer day.

Within a month, he was working late two or three times a week. On those occasions, he ate little for dinner and soon retreated to the living room. She'd find him seated on the sofa, pumping the buttons of a video game console and absorbed by the television screen. One evening, she interrupted his game to say they needed to go food shopping.

"Christ, I'm busting my ass to support us," he shot back. "Can't I have some free time to myself?"

"Ray, what's going on? Tell me the truth. I can't take this anymore."

He tossed the console aside and sprang up from the couch.

"You're not the only one who can't take it anymore. I want to have some fun in life, and that's not happening here."

She could feel the heat of his breath on her face, and the pupils of his eyes loomed large.

"Ray, are you on something?"

"That's it!" he yelled and lashed out so quickly she had no time to defend herself.

After the door slammed shut, she rolled over, and pain flared in her elbow where the skin had been scraped away by the carpet. She dragged herself to the bathroom and stared in the mirror. Her tear-stained face was unmarked. She ran some warm water in the sink, cleaned herself up, and put a Band-Aid on her arm.

Then she searched through the phone book. The woman who answered her call provided directions. Nicole gathered what they needed and dressed the baby. When the taxi came, the driver helped her carry the suitcases, stroller and collapsed crib down the stairs.

On her third day in the crowded shelter, she phoned home. Her mother and father arrived an hour later. Their we-told-you-so looks were on full display. In spite of that, it was a relief to walk into her old room. Once Julie was settled, Nicole shared a tea with her parents at the kitchen table and recounted the breakup with Raymond as she had rehearsed it.

Her mother's face was stoic. "You're welcome to stay here while you sort things out."

"We'll do what we can to help," her father added, as if on cue.

There was no question of reconciliation. Ray wanted out, and so did she. The possibility of continuing in school for several more years was closed off. There was now a child to support and no certainty regarding what financial help she might receive from him. Her parents' home provided a refuge for the time being, but she had to think beyond that. Acquiring a place of her own entailed finding a job, one that paid enough to cover the cost of childcare.

Someone at her dad's workplace mentioned his niece had been hired at an aerospace company on the west side of the island. He passed the name along. "It sounds like there might be other openings," her father said. "The money is more than you'd earn as a salesgirl or a secretary. You've got a child to think about now."

Nicole bit her tongue, thanked him for the tip, and promised to phone.

At the interview two days later, the middle-aged woman in Human Resources explained that Tanner and Ward was a UK-based company with installations worldwide. The Montreal plant specialized in the repair and overhaul of aircraft engines which powered commercial, corporate, and military jets.

Although her own English was good, Nicole was relieved the woman spoke to her only in French. It just made everything easier.

"On their arrival, the engines are dismantled," the woman said, "and the parts are cleaned, repaired, or replaced. After being reassembled and tested in cells that simulate flight conditions, they're shipped back to their owners.

"We recently hired the first female to work in the department where engine parts are cleaned. Does this sound like something you'd be interested in?"

Nicole started work at Tanner and Ward the following Monday. Each morning, she delivered Julie to a neighbour until her return in the late afternoon.

On her first day, she was introduced to Annie Desjardins. Everyone headed for the cafeteria at break time and settled into one of the long tables as a group. As Nicole walked towards them with her coffee, Annie motioned to an empty chair beside her and asked how she had ended up there. Nicole mentioned the tip from her father, without going into further details.

On the way back to their work area, they were trailing behind the others when Annie turned to her. "I really hope you like it here because since I started last week, I've been a bit lonely. Not that the guys are a problem. It's just…they're guys, you know, and everyone wants to check out 'the new girl.'" She pressed her lips together and shrugged her shoulders. "It's nice having another woman to hang out with."

That first encounter with Annie remained rooted in her memory almost two decades later.

# Chapter 3

Nicole glanced at the clock in the cafeteria and settled onto a chair. Still ten minutes before the start of her shift. She took a sip of coffee and looked up. Annie was scooting towards her.

"Nicole, have you heard?"

She set down her cup. "Heard what?"

"About Paul Dufour."

"What about him?"

"He's switched sides. The new head of training at Tanner and Ward. Can you believe it? It's bloody outrageous. If he walked in here right now, you'd have to hold me back," Annie said. "I swear on my mother's grave. I'd toss your coffee at him."

"I thought your mother was alive. And leave my coffee out of this."

Annie frowned, and her hand fluttered. "Don't quibble."

She stalked around the end of the table, yanked out the chair opposite Nicole, and plunked herself down. "I just bumped into Vincent Legault. He attended the emergency meeting where Dufour dropped his bombshell."

Annie imitated a little girl's voice. "*I hope no one will hold it against me for resigning as union president to take charge of the company's training program. My goal has always been to improve conditions for the employees, and that's what I'll continue to do in my new position.*"

"Yeah, right. The scumbag. And that's not all Vincent told me. Guess who's running to replace Dufour as union president?"

"No idea."

"Think protégé."

"Robert Simard?"

"We have a winner!"

Annie slapped the tabletop, and Nicole's coffee lapped the side of her cup. She picked it up and took another sip.

Annie leaned forward. "If Simard leads us into the next contract talks, the fix is in. He's not going to stand up to the company. His mentor is part of management now. That's why you need to run against him."

Nicole choked on her mouthful of coffee.

Annie shifted sideways to avoid the spray and rubbed a hand down her front. "Don't make me rethink this. You'll need to show more poise if you want to lead us into those talks."

Nicole wiped the back of a hand across her lips. "Has your anger kidnapped your brain? I'm not the person to replace Paul Dufour. I've never even been on the union executive."

Annie lowered her voice. "That's in your favour. You haven't been contaminated by all the schmoozing that's gone on between Dufour and management. You're an outsider who owes them nothing."

"I appreciate the endorsement, but that's way out of my league."

"Not true," Annie said. "You're low key. But there's no smoke and mirrors. People respect that."

# Chapter 4

Nicole joined several dozen colleagues who had driven over from the plant for the monthly union meeting in a basement room of the Holiday Inn on Côte-de-Liesse. The nomination of Paul Dufour's successor was on the agenda, prompting a larger turnout than usual. She settled herself in the back row and watched Robert Simard shaking hands and squeezing shoulders. If no one ran against him, he would be acclaimed on the spot.

The vice-president, Vincent Legault, was chairing the meeting and seated behind a table at the front of the room. Last Friday, he drew Nicole aside when she stopped by the union office to pick up a grievance form. "You're one of our most active stewards," he said. "Have you ever considered taking on more responsibility?"

"Like what?"

"Now that Dufour's resigned, the president's position is open. If we lose further ground under someone else's leadership, you could find yourself trying to defend people in the framework of a weakened contract. Do you want to risk that?"

"You're vice-president. Why don't you run?"

"My wife's ill, Nicole. This isn't the time."

"Sorry, Vincent. I didn't know. But I don't have the authority for that position."

"Don't underestimate yourself," he said.

Nicole noticed Annie bustle into the room and give her a wave before stopping to chat with Vincent. As their conversation ended, he called the meeting to order, and Annie sat down opposite him.

The usual reports followed, one after the other. Half an hour later, Nicole was struggling not to drift off when she heard Vincent say, "Next, we'll take nominations for the post of president."

She was blinking herself back into the meeting when a guy thrust his arm in the air, and Vincent recognized him. "I nominate Robert Simard."

"Further nominations? Going once, going twice."

Annie waved her hand, and Vincent turned to her.

"Nicole Fortin," she said.

At the sound of her name, Nicole straightened up in her chair.

"You've got to be kidding," someone said in the front row, and several heads jerked in her direction.

She stared back at them, all the while rubbing sweaty palms along her thighs.

"Order," Vincent said. "Any further nominations?"

No one spoke.

"Robert Simard, do you accept the nomination?"

Simard rose. "Yes, and I would like to thank my nominator." He turned and glanced her way before taking his seat.

"Nicole Fortin, do you accept the nomination?"

Annie nodded at her, and silence settled over the room as Nicole worked her way through jumbled thoughts.

"I...I do."

Annie broke into a grin.

"The voting will take place next week in the plant," Vincent said.

# Chapter 5

It was just after eight in the evening when they walked into the bar. Annie went in search of a table while Nicole retreated to the washroom. Despite a considerable effort to appear calm and composed, the last seven days had been nerve-wracking. It had taken years to get to a place where she felt good about herself again. She knew her limits. Agreeing to run for president went way beyond them. But if she said no, Robert Simard's coronation would be complete, and he'd take that as permission to do as he pleased. She couldn't let that happen. With no expectation of winning, she was hoping for enough support to put him on guard and not embarrass herself.

A tall, dark-haired waitress was strolling away by the time Nicole reached their table in the corner.

Annie stood up, removed her coat, and placed it on the back of her chair. "I ordered two glasses of red. That okay?"

Nicole nodded and wiped her damp hands on a serviette.

"My turn for the ladies' room," Annie said.

Nicole settled on a chair and glanced out the window. Early December snowflakes swayed across the cone of light from a nearby streetlamp and mimicked the motion in her stomach. She hadn't been this wound up for twenty years. Back then, she was perched on a starting block and staring into a fifty-metre pool, primed to swim her heart out against seven other women.

She was still fidgeting with the serviette and staring out the window when Annie manoeuvred into her chair.

"How long will it take for the results?" her friend asked.

"No idea. But the polls closed over an hour ago."

The waitress had just delivered their wine when her cell phone jingled.

"Can I speak with Nicole?" a raspy voice said.

"Yes. Who am I talking to?"

Annie leaned forward. "What happened?"

Nicole raised her hand with the palm outward.

"It's Donny Taylor from the balloting committee. We just finished the count. Congratulations."

The pounding in her chest echoed in her ears. "What…what did you say?"

"Congratulations, Nicole. You're the new president of Local 1210 of the Amalgamated Metalworkers Union."

She somehow managed to rotate her hand with the thumb pointing up.

"Yes!" Annie whooped. Two women sitting nearby stopped chatting and looked over at them.

After the call ended, Annie hugged her. "You did it."

Nicole leaned back in the chair and took a sip of wine. Her stomach churned.

"Hello! You won!"

She gulped down more wine. "It wasn't supposed to turn out this way. I only ran against him because no one else stepped forward."

Annie reached across and touched her forearm. "You'll do fine."

Nicole wasn't sure if her friend's words expressed hope or conviction.

An hour later, she left the bar and drove home, overwhelmed by the thought of how unprepared she was for whatever lay ahead. She lumbered up the stairs to the apartment and slid her key in the lock. Before Nicole could turn the knob, the door swung open.

"Congratulations, Mom!" Julie wrapped her in an embrace.

"How did you find out?"

Her daughter's eyes opened wide. "It's all over the local news."

"Yeah, right. Who told you?"

"Someone phoned here, and I gave him your cell number."

"I can't believe it. This is more than I bargained for."

Julie made a face. "Hey, you'll survive. Nineteen years with me, and you're still standing. Well, maybe leaning is more accurate, but what do you expect at your age." She broke into a smile and hugged her mother again. "I'm proud of you."

"Do I slouch?"

"Only to make sure you've buttoned your clothes and tied up your shoes."

Her daughter's smile widened. She was enjoying this, but Nicole wasn't in the mood. "I need to throw our laundry in the washer and make my lunch for tomorrow."

"You'll have to pick up the pace, madam president. I'm a step ahead of you." Julie pointed down the hallway. "I was just about to empty the dryer."

"I guess I owe you a sandwich for that. Salmon or tuna?"

"Either one," Julie said, "with some pickles on the side."

By the time Nicole finished the sandwiches, her body was signalling the need for rest, but her mind had missed the message. She checked the bathroom cabinet for a natural sedative but came up empty-handed. Half an hour later, she crawled under the covers and stared at the neon numbers on the bedside table until sleep finally conquered her.

# Chapter 6

Next morning, Nicole found herself stuck in rush-hour traffic on the Metropolitan Autoroute as it cut across the city like a jagged scar. She pulled into the front parking lot of Tanner and Ward in Ville Saint-Laurent twenty minutes later and gazed at the long, single-storey, white structure, its green sloping roof partially covered in glistening snow.

In front of the main entrance, Quebec and Canadian flags shook and shimmed from tall silver poles. Rising up behind the facade was the plant itself, a two-storey building of beige brick, topped by an array of vents and stacks in various shapes and sizes protruding from the tarred rooftop. While imposing from the front, the side view provided a better picture of how massive the structure was. It had been expanded multiple times over the years to handle the repair and overhaul of the company's gas turbine engines which powered a variety of aircraft.

Nicole shook her head. Hard to believe eighteen years had passed since her first day there in 1993. Back then, half of a hinged double gate at the eastern end of the complex remained open to allow employees access. A security guard stood beside it, observing those who entered. The gate had since disappeared, replaced by a remotely-controlled metal fence that slid open to allow vehicles through. Three enclosed turnstiles now handled pedestrian traffic, while guards tucked away in a basement room surveyed images from cameras trained on all the entrances.

The changes were part of a million-dollar security upgrade at the Montreal aerospace plant following the September 11 attacks a decade ago. The connection with these events south of the border seemed tenuous to Nicole at the time. But the repercussions were all too real. Instead of striding into work through an open gate as in the past, employees swiped identity cards under the watchful gaze of security cameras, then pushed past metal turnstiles. Going into work felt like incarceration.

Nicole eased herself out of the car and grabbed a grey backpack from the rear seat. The sprinkle of overnight snow was already melting as she made her way across the parking lot, swiped her card at the turnstile, and passed through the narrow metal cocoon.

When she walked into the second-floor changing room, Annie was seated on a wooden bench between two rows of lockers, lacing up her work boots.

"Hey, look who's here," her friend said.

Nicole moseyed over to the bench and dropped her backpack with a thud.

Annie studied her for a moment. "Not at your most charming this early in the morning, especially with the weight of the world on those shoulders. Brighten up buttercup. Catch you in the caf."

After changing into her work clothes, Nicole stopped by the union bulletin board next to the cafeteria where the election results were posted: Nicole Fortin, 338; Robert Simard, 312. Eighty per cent of the eight hundred members had cast a ballot, and the vote was almost evenly split.

A voice behind her said, "Congratulations."

She spun around and found herself facing Simard, bookended by a couple of his buddies. He didn't extend his hand, and his eyes narrowed.

"I'll be around to pick up the pieces when this is all over. You can count on that."

He brushed by her and entered the lunchroom.

# Chapter 7

On her first day of work at Tanner and Ward, Nicole had been assigned to a department called the wash. As she entered the area, her stomach fluttered at the heavy metallic smell. "The longer you're here, the less you notice it," Annie told her.

The main plant ran the length of three football fields and contained several different engine lines. The wash was stuck in a corner of the shop behind high brick walls and thick plastic doors. Here jet engine parts were cleaned in rows of large tanks containing different chemicals.

Protection from the toxic solvents used to degrease and clean the parts required wearing yellow rubber gloves and sleeves, full-body aprons, safety glasses and masks, or plastic face shields. Nicole's colleagues looked like medical personnel treating highly infectious patients.

All the gear weighed her down, slowing her movements and sapping her energy. Despite the safety precautions, accidents happened. She was paired with a guy named Luc, who showed her a nasty scar on his inner arm, the residue of a nitric acid burn.

Back in the women's locker room at the end of her shift, Nicole slipped off her work shirt and sniffed a sleeve. "Geez, I stink."

Annie grinned. "Welcome to our kerosene world. It's a great cleaning agent, but it does leave its calling card. Get used to it. Your clothes and skin will smell like that after every shift. Hop in the shower, use lots of soap, and bring a change of clothes tomorrow morning. That'll help."

Nicole soon became accustomed to the background hum of the ventilation system. But the clamour of high-pressure hoses and air-powered guns used to clean and dry the parts forced her to wear hearing protection most of the time. Whenever the ventilation shut down, an alarm was triggered, and everyone had to evacuate the area. Only emergency crews equipped with oxygen were allowed in until the problem was solved.

With the aid of various chains and pulleys, Nicole lifted, lowered, twisted, and turned heavy engine parts throughout the day. By the end of her fourth shift, she struggled to remove her clothes in the locker room. A spider web of pain radiated across her shoulders and down her back. That night, she ran a hot bath, added Epsom salts, and soaked in the tub until she caught herself drifting off. When the alarm sounded at five o'clock the next morning, she almost called it quits, but managed to pry her eyelids open and stagger from the bedroom.

After a month of being toughened by the work, and convinced she would survive, Nicole put a down payment on a ten-year-old Toyota. The move saved her an hour of daily travelling time and made getting around with a young child more manageable.

Six weeks later, she rented a place on Casgrain Avenue in the Villeray neighbourhood, only a twenty-minute commute from Tanner and Ward. It was on the top floor of a duplex. A winding staircase rose from the street to the second-floor landing. Reaching her new lodgings turned out to be a workout in itself, especially with Julie in hand, but was worth the effort.

The back balcony faced west and was bathed in sunshine from noon till nightfall. Her apartment sat next to a quiet cross street. The living room, a bedroom, and the kitchen ran off the hallway to the right, with windows facing north. This gave the place an airy brightness, rather than the feel of being cooped up in a tunnel. The white walls had been freshly painted, and the lightly toned wooden floors and baseboards shone in the sunlight that entered through the windows. Mature maple and ash trees lined both sides of the street below, providing a canopy of shade.

Nicole spent the next few weeks visiting discount furniture stores and used appliance outlets in the area until she'd furnished the place. The crowning touch was a refurbished coffee machine that brewed a strong enough cup to get her out of the apartment each weekday morning in time to drop Julie at daycare and make it in by seven o'clock.

The apartment was more mix and match than IKEA showroom, but it provided the independence she needed. After living in unfamiliar territory with Raymond, escaping to a temporary shelter, then enduring the iciness of her parents' home, she finally found herself in a place where she could relax and breathe.

The sole person she answered to was Julie. Her favourite time of day was following dinner when she pushed other concerns aside and spent time with her daughter. Once the child was bathed and settled for the night, Nicole cleaned up the dishes and prepared the next day's lunch. Then she toppled into bed until a beeping alarm shattered her sleep the following morning.

With the help of others, she learned how to clean an expanding range of engine parts, and her confidence grew. But she was unprepared for what lay ahead when spring segued into summer. Despite a few large fans mounted on the walls, the lack of air conditioning made working in the wash like toiling in a sauna.

At the end of each shift, she plodded back to the locker room, slumped down on the bench, then wriggled out of sweat-soaked garments and stumbled into the shower. Though bigger and stronger than Nicole, Annie was less fit, and the heat took its toll on her as well. Alone they might have wilted, but together they survived.

As the days rolled into weeks, and the weeks into months, their friendship deepened. Annie fed her updates on the latest escapades of her two preadolescent sons, while Nicole shared Julie's evolution from baby to little girl.

One morning, a young male worker strode by their table in the cafeteria. Annie's gaze wandered as she followed his progress toward the coffee machines. Nicole waved her hand and snapped her fingers. "Hey, didn't your parents teach you not to stare?"

Annie ignored her for a moment. "Nice ass," she said.

"Such language from a married woman and mother of two."

Annie gave her a look. "Don't pretend you didn't notice. If you're feeling lonely, ignored, and horny, a one-night stand might be right for you. Side effects may include bruised lips, sore hips, and squeezed tits. You may also experience anxiety, insomnia, mood swings, depression, self-loathing, and suicidal thoughts after the act. But remember, you only live once. Consult your best friend if you think a one-night stand might be right for you." She arched her eyebrows.

The next day, during morning break, their colleague Luc joined them. While they sipped coffee, he displayed the latest acid burn on his arm and recited the list of injuries he'd suffered, from a broken finger to a pulled back muscle and a sprained ankle.

"I don't know if you're aware of this," he said, "but when you two first appeared on the scene, some of the guys wagered on how long you'd last. Most gave you a few days. They didn't think women would stick it out. People respect you for hanging tough, even the guys who lost the bet."

# Chapter 8

Nicole returned to the union office and turned on her computer. While the machine powered up, she recalled her conversation with Julie the previous day. She was setting the table for dinner when her daughter asked if she'd lost weight.

"It's one of the perks that comes with my new position."

"You look tired," Julie said. "Are you sleeping well?"

"Who appointed you medical supervisor?"

"Seriously Mom, you've only been union president for a few weeks, and the negotiations haven't even begun. You can't run yourself into the ground over this stuff."

She knew her daughter was right. But what she proposed was easier said than done. Today mirrored the others preceding it. A union member in component repair was sent home and suspended after an altercation with a foreman. An assembler suffered a hand injury on the T24 engine line and required medical treatment. His workmates accused management of ignoring safety procedures in an effort to speed up production. The company's health insurer had begun refusing claims for diagnostic tests always accepted in the past. A failure to reverse this new policy could cost people hundreds of dollars each.

Nicole had spent half the day dealing with these issues and the rest of her time sketching out a schedule to meet with each union committee in preparation for the pending negotiations. She was about to begin wading through a dozen emails cluttering her inbox when she became aware of someone's presence.

Alex McCarthy was standing at the entrance to her office, his hands resting on the door frame.

"How are you, Nicole?"

"At the moment, I feel like a juggler with one arm tied behind my back and too many balls in the air."

He smiled and shut the door.

She watched as he eased himself into a chair. "Thanks for agreeing to meet me after your shift. Hard day?"

"Tougher than twenty years ago," he said. "Recovery time takes longer." He massaged the back of his neck. "To what do I owe the honour?"

Nicole liked the lingering trace of an Irish accent, the melodic lilt of his speech. He'd worked as an engine assembler at Tanner and Ward for more than thirty years.

"Alex, I'm going to be posting an announcement for elections to the negotiating committee. Nominations are next Tuesday, and the vote takes place the following week. There are two positions open on the committee alongside the president. I've been talking to people about possible candidates, and your name's come up on more than one occasion. I wondered if you'd consider standing. We could use your experience."

He stroked his chin. "You might be after the wrong man, Nicole. There's someone else who seems eager to join you on the negotiating committee."

"Who would that be?"

"He made a visit to our department this afternoon, said he'd bring experience to a committee that's too green. One of the lads looked him in the eye and said he preferred green to mush because green could ripen, but mush was tasteless. Brother Simard got the message and wandered off looking for support elsewhere."

There was the trace of a smile before his expression grew serious.

"As for me standing, you're raising a big question. I haven't held any position in the union for quite some time. And to tell you the truth, since my wife passed away last year, the cloud hasn't lifted." He looked away and brushed at a pant leg.

"If you don't feel ready to jump back in, that's understandable," Nicole said, "perfectly understandable. On the other hand, maybe it would help lift that cloud a little. I know you've had your share of disagreements with Paul Dufour in the past, but you have strong opinions, and you're not afraid to express them. We're going to need people like that on the negotiating committee."

He stared at the floor and made no move to speak.

"The race between Robert and me was close," she added. "It's no secret that he and many others don't think I'm fit for the job. He might even be right. I promise to throw everything I have into this, but I'll need help."

Alex passed a hand through salt and pepper hair that had seen thicker days and eyed her for a moment. "Let me get back to you, Nicole." He pulled his lean frame from the chair.

"Sure. Give it some thought, Alex. I'd look forward to working with you. Thanks for coming by."

He nodded and disappeared through the doorway.

She had been expecting more of a discussion on the subject, but at least he hadn't said no. It was hard to gauge from this exchange whether he'd agree to stand for the committee. Nicole hoped she hadn't appeared too desperate. He was a handful when he got riled up. But there was no one she would rather have sitting beside her at the bargaining table.

# Chapter 9

Nicole posted the results of the negotiating committee election on the union bulletin board. Then she slipped into the cafeteria for a quick bite to eat. Simon Arnaud walked through the doorway. She waved to get his attention, and he approached her table, a plastic container in his hand.

"Let me heat this up," he said and joined the line of those waiting for a microwave.

By the time he returned, she was halfway through her toasted western sandwich. He peeled the lid off the container, and steam escaped.

"What is that?"

He tilted it towards her. "Leftovers from last night. A Haitian staple."

Chunks of chicken, onion, and pepper peeked out from a reddish sauce mixed with rice. A tangy aroma of garlic and tomato tickled her nostrils. "Smells good. Did you make it?"

His lips widened into a smile. "No. That's my wife's doing. I know my way around the kitchen, but Joëlle's the expert."

After he sat down, she extended her hand. "Congratulations, Simon, and welcome to the negotiating committee."

"Thanks, Nicole. I didn't expect to be elected along with Alex McCarthy. I figured Robert Simard was more likely to win than me. I guess the hard feelings he expressed after his loss in the presidential race cost him support. Some people questioned his ability to work with you on the bargaining committee."

Simon grabbed the salt and sprinkled some on his meal. "Albert Lavoie also deserves his share of credit."

Nicole frowned and cocked her head. "The machine shop foreman who retired a couple of years ago?"

"That's the one."

"What's he got to do with this?"

"Well, when I first started as a welder, he took a dislike to me. I wasn't sure why and wondered if it was a racial thing. Then I noticed how friendly he was with a brother from Jamaica. So I figured that couldn't be it.

"During my third week on the job, I made a mistake and ruined a part because the scheme I was working with hadn't been updated. It wasn't my fault, but Lavoie threatened to let me go. I went to the senior welder, who stood up for me and got the shop committee involved. The union couldn't file a grievance on my behalf since I was on probation, but some dust was kicked up, and Lavoie backed off. The committee later discovered I had been offered the job over one of his nephews. He'd been looking for a way to reverse that."

Simon stirred his food with a fork. "A few months after I finished probation, a steward's position opened up in the department. I'd never given much thought to unions before my run-in with Lavoie but put my name forward and was elected."

Nicole swallowed the last of her sandwich and wiped her lips with a serviette. "Fancy that. I never pictured old Albert Lavoie as a union recruiter."

Simon had just squeaked by Simard in the three-person race, but Nicole was pleased he'd been elected. His calmness would help bring some balance to the committee.

# Chapter 10

Today would be the first time Nicole had been in a meeting with Paul Dufour since he resigned as union president. Some considered his action a betrayal, while others thought he had just taken advantage of a chance to better himself. But if he had decided to switch sides, who would be next? Nicole knew that was on people's minds. Management was always on the lookout for promising individuals who could be lured over with offers of supervisory positions. Dufour wasn't the first to make this move and wouldn't be the last. Every time that happened, the union's credibility took a hit.

He was launching a new cross-training program, and she had asked to attend the session. Getting a peek at a proposal that would likely feature in the upcoming negotiations could prove useful.

As she passed by the Orion engine line, an inspector wearing hearing protection was busy engraving a serial number on a casing with an air-powered tool. The screeching whine of metal on metal assaulted her eardrums. She rooted around in her pockets for foam earplugs without success. After she turned the corner, the shrill beeping of a forklift serenaded her as it backed along the aisle in her direction, dragging a T24 engine on its wheeled stand. By the time she entered the training room, her ears were ringing.

Two dozen machinists were seated on folding chairs. Marcel Bégin saluted her. He was approaching retirement now but had probably trained half the men in this room on various machines over the years.

"Hey, what are you doing here?" he said. "Checking up on your old friend, Dufour?"

"No. I'm here to keep an eye on you."

He grinned and swept the palm of his hand towards an empty seat three over from his own.

Paul Dufour strode into the room and laid a file folder on the front desk. He was sporting grey slacks and a white dress shirt rather than the blue uniform worn by shop floor employees. His coiffed brown hair looked shorter than before. He glanced Nicole's way and nodded, then refocused on those before him.

"Since this is the first in a series of departmental meetings I'll be leading on cross-training, the union asked to attend for informational purposes. I have no problem with that," he said. "If I were still in Nicole's position, I would've made the same request. After all, need to keep an eye on these slippery management types."

A few people smiled back.

"Well, it looks like I'm not the only one who stayed up late last night watching the hockey game. Too bad it took overtime and a shootout to end it. We'd all be more rested if they'd settled matters in regulation."

"That's okay," a familiar voice said. "If you just keep it down, we can catch a few Z's right here."

Heads turned toward Marcel Bégin, and Dufour grinned. "I'd like to accommodate you, Marcel, but I'm going to need your attention for the next few minutes. However, if your stomach agrees, you can grab a few winks during the lunch break."

"Fat chance," someone said. "Bégin needs the full thirty minutes to finish off that feast he totes to the lunchroom every day."

Marcel glanced over his shoulder. "Hard work takes energy, and energy needs to be replaced."

"Hard work? Give me a break," came the reply. "You don't remember what that feels like."

Dufour waited for the laughter to settle. "Well, I don't want to keep any of you from your lunch period, so let's move on. The purpose of our meeting is to discuss cross-training. We have a lot of skill and experience in this group, but we need to spread it around. Take Fred, for example. He's the man when it comes to a job on any of the grinding machines in the shop. He knows all the tricks and could do the work with his eyes closed."

"Sometimes he does," Marcel said. "That's where your scrap comes from."

Fred turned to Marcel and gave him the finger.

After the reaction died away, Dufour continued. "But sometimes the priority job involves a lathe or a milling machine, which Fred may be less familiar with. We need to provide the training so he can work on the priority job, instead of doing something less urgent on a grinding machine. I know this will take time. But in the long run, cross-training is in our interest, both as a company and as individuals.

"I'll pass around some sheets listing every machine in the shop. I want you to indicate your level of conversancy on each one. Based on that, we'll develop a training program. Any questions?"

A hand shot up.

"Yeah, Max."

"Are we going to have any say in which machines we're trained on?"

"Once we have an idea of what everyone's already capable of doing, we'll come up with proposals for who is trained on what machines."

Someone raised an arm in the front row.

"If we're going to be learning additional jobs, can we expect extra pay?"

"You should probably discuss that with Nicole rather than me," Dufour said. "Listen, we're in a very competitive environment. Some companies are ahead of us on the learning curve. And new places are opening up in other parts of the world where wages and benefits are a fraction of what they are here. The more efficient we become, the better our chances of keeping the work in this plant. Cross-training will make you more productive, and hopefully, more secure in your jobs.

"Any other questions?" He scanned the room. "If not, fill out these forms, pass them on to me, and you're free to go. Thanks for your attention. I look forward to working with each of you."

Nicole was walking behind Fred as they filed out. He leaned in toward Dufour and handed him the form. "You remember how hard it is to teach an old dog new tricks?"

Dufour nodded.

"Well, I'm an old dog. Keep that in mind."

He wasn't smiling.

# Chapter 11

Nicole squeezed into the right-hand lane of rush-hour traffic as it spasmed eastward along the Metropolitan Autoroute. After she took the exit for Saint Laurent Boulevard, the wailing of a fire truck forced her to pull over. As she watched it speed by, Marc was in her head.

When she first bumped into him, Julie had just turned four. They were at the supermarket, and Julie was trying to reach for some cookies while Nicole's back was turned. When she looked around, this guy with curly hair and a stunning smile was handing her daughter the package. Julie was gazing up at him like she couldn't believe it. Who was this man, and where did he come from?

When Marc realized Nicole was her mother, he said, "She knows what she wants. Which parent does she take after?"

"Julie only has a mom in her life."

Before she knew what was happening, Nicole had agreed to meet him for coffee.

Six weeks later, Marc had a four-day weekend off from the fire hall. A friend of his had raved about a recent camping trip. So along with Julie, they headed south through the Eastern Townships, crossed over the border to Vermont and skirted Lake Champlain. The sun beat down from a cloudless sky, and a light breeze wrapped them in the fragrance of midsummer. They rambled along roads bordered by thick forests, past farms with fields that stretched on forever, and through villages boasting small general stores.

At the state park, they set up a tent. Julie had never camped out before and was wide-eyed at the prospect. They made their way up the mountain trail, with Julie on Marc's shoulders. At the top, he wrapped her in his arms, and all three climbed up the fire tower. They oohed and awed at the lake, forests, and fields below. Nicole asked another couple to take a photo of them with the view in the background.

By the time they made it back to their tent, the sun was beginning its descent. They caught their breath, headed down to the changing rooms by the beach, and hit the lake for a swim. After dinner, they roasted marshmallows and marvelled at the starry sky. The next morning, they rented a canoe and took a tour of the lake.

Shortly after, Marc moved in, and Julie had a father for the first time in her memory. As the weeks slipped into months, Nicole became convinced she had found someone special, a man who wanted to be with her and treated her daughter as his own.

One evening, after Julie had been tucked in for the night, they were curled up on the living room couch when Marc surprised her.

"Would you consider having another child?"

It was the first time he'd raised the question, though the thought had been bouncing around in her brain for weeks.

She looked up at him. "Is that what you want?"

"Yeah."

"It's a big step."

"Let's do it," he said.

But they never did.

The weekend Marc raised the idea of a brother or sister for Julie, he gave Nicole a pair of earrings with overlapping hearts. She showed them to Annie during their break on Monday morning and mentioned she'd never been happier.

"Tell me something I don't know," Annie said. "Your smile to frown ratio has been off the charts for months."

The week flew by for Nicole. Saturday night, she dozed off on the couch, waiting for Marc to return from his shift at the fire hall. When she opened her eyes, it was past one o'clock. She retreated to the bedroom and snuggled under the covers. He had told her that if he were ever late, not to worry. It only meant his shift had been extended because of a call.

Nicole thought she was dreaming when she first heard a ringing noise. She rolled over, and all seemed quiet, so she drifted off again. The second time it woke her, and she squinted at the alarm clock. It was four-thirty in the morning. She scrambled out of bed, hurried to the kitchen and picked up the telephone. After clearing her throat, she managed to say hello.

"Can I speak with Nicole Fortin," a woman's voice said.

"Yes. What do you want?" Now she was wide awake and massaged her forehead with the fingers of her free hand.

"I'm calling from Notre Dame Hospital on Sherbrooke Street East. Marc Lapointe has been admitted here, and you are listed as next of kin."

"Yes, he's my companion. What happened to him?"

"I'm sorry, I don't have further information on his condition at this time, but please identify yourself to the person on duty at the emergency department when you arrive."

Nicole thanked the woman for her call, then rushed to the bathroom, threw water on her face and changed into her street clothes. She roused Julie, but her daughter kept nodding off as Nicole tried to dress her. She tossed some items in a shoulder bag and dashed down the stairs with Julie in her arms.

There was little traffic as she drove south, racing through a series of green lights. At the hospital, she was met by a doctor who escorted her into a small room. He asked her to sit down and then explained that Marc had not survived emergency surgery.

She blinked back at him and opened her mouth to speak but was unable to make a sound. Her throat was parched, and the doctor offered her some water. She was still holding Julie, who was dosing, her head resting on Nicole's shoulder. If it hadn't been for her daughter's presence, she would have fallen to pieces then and there.

Nicole later learned that Marc had been driving home from his shift at the fire hall when a car with three teenage boys returning from a late-night party shot through a red light.

When she failed to show up for work on Monday, Annie phoned her. Nicole was still in shock. On hearing the news, Annie drove straight to the apartment. She called her husband, told him she would spend the night, and slept on the living room couch.

At the funeral a few days later, Nicole's parents said she and Julie were welcome to stay with them for a while. She declined their offer with thanks, knowing she needed to grieve on her own. Annie returned to the apartment and helped prepare dinner, then cleaned up the dishes while Nicole put Julie to bed.

"Are you sure you want to spend tonight alone?" Annie asked. "I can stay over again. Hugo will look after the boys."

Nicole shook her head. "Thanks for everything."

After Annie left, Nicole made herself some tea and moved into the living room. She rocked back and forth, staring into nothingness. A week ago, her life had never been better. Now it lay in ruins. How could that happen so suddenly? It all seemed surreal. Then she recalled her conversation with Marc on that very couch. And everything came pouring out.

She would never again experience the playfulness of his eyes and the flash of a boyish smile, the sound of his voice and the feel of his skin against her own. Overnight, her multi-coloured world turned monochrome, and the weight on her chest made breathing an effort.

Aside from her own sense of loss, the hardest part was explaining to Julie that Marc would no longer carry her on his shoulders when they walked through Jean-Talon Market on a Saturday afternoon. She would never again hop up and down, laughing and turning in circles, as he chased her underwater at the shallow end of the public pool, or be tucked into bed by him and receive a kiss on the forehead after being read one of her favourite stories.

In the days that followed, Nicole found herself taking refuge in the century-old Catholic Church nearby. She was not a religious person, despite her mother's best efforts, but found solitude inside the building's massive doors, which remained open during the day. Slumped on a pew in the subdued light of the airy interior, she discovered a space for undisturbed reflection, somewhere to try and make sense of it all, though she never succeeded.

When she returned to work, the sympathetic comments of others only reinforced her sense of loss. With Marc's death, a significant part of her life had been lopped off, and his absence was always present.

One day, a manager stopped beside her workstation to speak with the supervisor. After squeezing by them with an engine part, she caught the hint of a familiar scent from the man's cologne and spent the rest of her day in a fog.

With the exception of Annie, she tried to avoid social interaction and withdrew into her work. The focus of her life narrowed to her daughter. Nothing else mattered.

# Chapter 12

A year after Marc's death, the company posted openings for six apprentices to train as inspectors. Nicole applied, along with Annie, and both were accepted. They spent the next year taking courses at an aeronautical trade school, followed by eight months of in-plant training on the Adventus engine line.

They stamped documents for any work completed, and if there were ever an accident involving an engine part they had certified, a paper trail would lead back to them. Despite the added responsibility, inspecting parts proved more interesting than working in the wash. Besides that, the conditions were less onerous, and the pay was better.

One year later, the September 11 attacks sent airline travel into a tailspin. With many planes grounded, scheduled engine overhauls dropped off at Tanner and Ward, and layoffs began. Annie and Nicole were spared, but two men junior to them, Jean-Pierre and Étienne, were both sent home.

Nicole had helped train Jean-Pierre when he transferred into the department. One day he showed her several photos of his wife and their three children. Everyone seemed so happy. Nicole was envious. If she and Marc had been able to follow through on their plan, a child of theirs would have been about the same age as Jean-Pierre's youngest.

A month after the layoffs, overtime was posted. Some of her workmates were pleased to see it return and signed up. Ten days later, during lunch, Nicole pushed a photocopy of the weekly overtime sheet across the table to Annie.

"Look at this. With eighty-six hours of overtime being worked, why are Jean-Pierre and Étienne still on layoff?"

Annie counted the hours. "Maybe it's a one-off thing."

"No. I checked last week too. It was eighty-four hours. There's enough work to recall the guys, but if people keep working overtime, they won't be back."

"So, what do you propose?"

Nicole glanced across the cafeteria at a group of male colleagues who were eating together. She pointed in their direction. "Let's see what they think."

The two women picked up their lunch and walked over to the men.

"Hi, guys. Can we discuss something with you?"

"Sure, pull up a chair."

Nicole showed them the overtime sheet and explained this was the second week in a row with more than eighty hours posted. "Does it seem right Jean-Pierre and Étienne are still on layoff with this kind of overtime?"

She noticed embarrassed looks from two of the men whose names appeared on the sheet. As they walked back from lunch, the discussion continued. By the time they reached the department, there was agreement that those who had signed up for overtime would remove their names.

"We've got to speak with everyone on all three shifts," Nicole said. "I'm willing to stay late and talk with guys on second shift, but I can't come in early tomorrow morning and speak to those on nights before they leave. I have to drop my daughter off at school. Can anyone do that?"

Two of the men volunteered, and another offered to help her with the afternoon shift. Their efforts paid off. Everyone removed their names from the overtime list, and it was decided no one would volunteer until the two men were recalled.

When the foreman noticed names had been stroked off the list and no one else had signed up, he made some inquiries, then talked to the manager who had announced the decision to lay off the men. A departmental meeting was called. The manager explained the layoff was necessary because of the decline in work following the September 11 attacks. After he finished speaking, several heads turned in Nicole's direction. It took an effort to pry her lips apart.

"You've posted more than eighty hours of overtime in this department for the last two weeks," she said. "That's enough work to justify recalling Jean-Pierre and Étienne."

"Look, production has picked up recently," the manager said. "I'm not denying that. But it's too early to say if this will continue. When we need them, they'll be recalled. In the meantime, we have to cover the extra work in the shop. If we don't, it'll be sent elsewhere and only prolong their absence."

Annie glanced at Nicole as they headed to their workstations. "He turned that back on us pretty well."

"We're not beaten yet."

"What about the threat to move the work elsewhere if we don't do it?"

"Listen," Nicole said, "if people sign up for the overtime, management wins, and our guys lose. We need to stick together on this."

Annie eyed her for a moment. "Okay, I'm with you. But we have to convince everyone else."

Nicole nodded. "If you can come in early tomorrow and speak with those on nights, I'll talk to the guys on second shift before the manager meets with them this afternoon."

"You're really into this, aren't you," Annie said.

Nicole turned to her. "I can't get the photos of Jean-Pierre's kids out of my head."

When the overtime sheet was posted two days later with ninety hours offered, no one signed up. Before the end of the shift, all members of the department were called to a meeting. They were informed the company was invoking a clause in the collective agreement allowing it to impose up to eight hours of overtime a month on each employee.

Everyone was forced in for an extra shift. Three weeks later, the company had gone through the entire department with no one left to assign. Another meeting was called. The manager announced that a revised assessment of the workload meant the laid-off men would be returning. Following their shift, a group of them celebrated in a nearby bar. Everyone knew the men were coming back because they had stuck together.

A few weeks later, several of the guys approached Nicole to run for shop steward in the department. After giving it some thought, she agreed and was elected.

That was a decade ago. She should be accustomed to taking on management by now. But it wasn't the case. Every time a new dispute arose, she had to brace herself, and the fear of falling short never left her.

# Chapter 13

Nicole had just returned to the office following lunch in the cafeteria when her phone rang. Martin Goyette congratulated her on being elected union president and proposed a meeting so they could "get to know one another." She already knew him well enough. During his tenure as company president, management had increased probation from three months to six, doubling the time new employees were excluded from the health care and pension plans. But Goyette's call caught her by surprise. So she convened a meeting of the union executive and asked for advice on how to handle the encounter.

"When Paul Dufour was union president, he met Goyette from time to time," Vincent Legault said. "The rest of the executive had no idea what went on in those meetings. There was no accountability on Dufour's part. If we asked questions, he became defensive. We can't fall into that trap again."

Following their discussion, Nicole phoned Goyette and explained that she would be accompanied by the vice-president, Vincent Legault.

"I already know Vincent," he said. "It's you I'd like to chat with."

"Our policy is that no union officer meets with company representatives alone."

"Why is that?" he asked.

"So there's always a witness to whatever exchange takes place."

"Are you saying you don't trust me?"

"I'm saying the union executive wants to ensure accountability on the part of its representatives, so we've adopted this policy."

There was an awkward pause. "Could you hold for a moment, Nicole?" When he returned, his tone had softened. "Let's put this proposal aside. Would you and your negotiating committee be available for an introductory meeting with members of the company's committee next Friday at two o'clock?"

# Chapter 14

Accompanied by the other committee members, Nicole made the five-minute walk from the union office in the bowels of the plant to the corporate conference room at the front of the building. She wore a white union T-shirt bearing the Amalgamated Metalworkers logo.

As they entered the room, Goyette rose and offered his hand to each of them in turn. He gestured towards a waist-high credenza and invited them to have a tea or coffee. Nicole declined the offer, took her seat, and noticed several familiar faces sitting across from her.

Once everyone was settled in soft leather chairs, Goyette resumed his place at the head of the long oak table. "Shall we begin?" he said. "Since this is the first meeting between management and union representatives who will be working together in these negotiations, I've asked the union president, Nicole Fortin, to introduce the members of her committee, and then I will do so for the company." He nodded towards her.

Nicole turned to those opposite. "Let me begin by introducing our business agent, Daniel Leduc, to my right. He works out of our regional union office and services several other locals in the aerospace industry. We're confident his knowledge of conditions elsewhere will be helpful in these talks. Next to Daniel is Simon Arnaud, a shop steward who has worked at Tanner and Ward for the past fifteen years as a welder. And on my left is Alex McCarthy, an engine assembler for thirty-six years, who brings a good deal of experience to our team."

Following her introductions, Goyette clasped his hands together and smiled. "Thank you, Nicole. On behalf of the company, may I say we look forward to a fruitful exchange with you and the members of your committee. While we have our respective points of view to present, I hope none of us will lose sight of the fact we are involved in a common enterprise here. We operate in an increasingly competitive environment which will challenge every one of us. Our goal is to see the company prosper and have our employees share in that prosperity.

"In addition to myself, let me introduce the other members of our committee." He gestured to his right. "At the far end of the table, it's my pleasure to present André Turcotte, our vice-president in charge of production. Next to him is Charles Allard, the director of Human Resources. And finally, let me welcome Sophie Martel, who has recently joined us as senior legal counsel."

Martel acknowledged the attention directed her way with a sparkling smile. Pale blue eyes and a generous mouth nestled beneath honey-brown hair in a face of unlined skin.

Nicole noticed admiring stares from both sides of the table.

# Chapter 15

Martin Goyette stuffed the latest financial figures into his briefcase and wished his secretary Louise Durocher a pleasant weekend. He strolled down the hallway and through the main doors to the front parking lot of Tanner and Ward. Sunlight reflected off the black BMW roadster in his reserved parking space. Now that the ice and snow of winter had passed, there was no longer a layer of corrosive salt to worry about, just the residue of potholes to avoid. Having his favourite car back on the road lifted his spirits.

On the way home, he assessed the meeting with the union negotiating committee, which had concluded an hour ago. This would be the first time dealing with Nicole Fortin in contract talks. Paul Dufour had proven able to rise above his union position and view matters in a broader framework, including the needs of the company and the challenges of the market. Hopefully, Nicole could be persuaded to do the same.

Mutually understood realities were always preferable to threats as a way of reaching agreement. It was not a question of greed when profitable companies sought greater cost savings or increased productivity from their employees. These were dictated by the need to defend and expand market share. If a company wasn't competitive, there would be negative consequences for the workforce. That point had to be understood.

Under his guidance, the firm's profitability had improved in recent years. Based on that success, there had been lengthy discussions with Sir Edmund and the executive team in London about implementing further changes at the Montreal plant, which could then be used as a blueprint for future negotiations in other parts of the world. That made these talks tricky.

There was also another factor to consider. Thanks to generous government subsidies at both the provincial and federal levels, eight years of effort had gone into a project at the Montreal site which would lead to the creation of a new engine outside the UK for the first time in Tanner and Ward's history. Any delay in this work caused by the local negotiations would have international repercussions. On the other hand, launching the engine on schedule, and concluding successful contract talks under his leadership, could be crowned by a promotion to the company's head office in London.

Martin Goyette pulled into the driveway of the two-storey, red brick house which was bathed in the slanting rays of a descending sun. He drove by Claire's sedan, flicked open the garage door and slid in beside his silver Mercedes.

Pilar was poking at a roast in the oven when he stepped into the kitchen. Her head jerked in his direction.

"Oh, hello, Mr. Goyette. How are you?"

"I'm excellent, Pilar. How about you?"

"Everything is fine. Dinner will be ready in thirty minutes."

"It smells delicious. Is Mrs. Goyette home?"

"Yes. I think she is upstairs."

He walked through the dining room and bounded up the winding staircase to the second floor. In the master bedroom, Claire was poised before the full-length mirror. She was wearing her undergarments and holding up a black strapless gown.

"Hello, darling."

She turned and greeted him with a dazzling smile.

The first time he saw her at a cousin's wedding, his jaw dropped, and a relentless pursuit began. She had relinquished a highly successful career in advertising to raise their son and daughter, both of whom were now off at university. In recent years, she had begun lending her expertise to several philanthropic foundations where her services were in demand.

He placed his hands on her waist, kissed her cheek, and found himself enveloped in her scent.

"I'm trying to decide what I should wear tomorrow night," she said. "What do you think?"

"Oh, yes, the charity ball for the Children's Hospital. You'll look smashing, especially next to the handsome gentleman in the matching black tuxedo." He winked, and she laughed.

"Everyone will be there," she said. "What an opportunity to network for future fundraising projects."

As she hung the dress in a closet, he walked over and locked the bedroom door. When she turned around, he guided her to the bed and laid her down.

She stared up at him. "You know, dessert should always follow the main course, dear."

"Why not break with protocol this evening?" he said. "We have half an hour before dinner is served."

She pursed her lips. "All right, let's be naughty."

Thirty minutes later, he poured spoonfuls of dark gravy over thin slices of roast beef, as his stomach growled.

## Chapter 16

The day before negotiations were to open with the company, Julie and Nicole joined several hundred people for a noisy demonstration in their neighbourhood in solidarity with the ongoing student strike against proposed tuition fee hikes at the province's universities. The marchers, ranging in age from toddlers to grandparents, banged pots and blew whistles. "What a blast to see such a mix of local people in the streets," Nicole told her daughter.

The broadening support for the students during the past couple of months had created a growing belief that those in authority could be challenged, and change was possible. As May drew to a close, there was a palpable sense of resistance in the air.

Over the previous weeks, the union committee had spent endless hours reviewing every clause in the collective agreement. Armed with feedback from a questionnaire on the members' priorities in the negotiations, and aided by a review of recent settlements at other aerospace companies, a package of proposals had been presented and adopted at a special union meeting.

The company's bottom line had improved significantly, thanks in part to concessions wrung from the workforce in recent years. This time around, people were hoping to make gains, and the union negotiators were expected to deliver. Nicole had explained countless times that the outcome of these talks rested on the shoulders of eight hundred members, not four individuals, but there was no denying the pressure her committee was under.

A young woman in a charcoal jacket and white top greeted Nicole with a smile at the reception desk of the hotel off Cavendish Boulevard where the talks were scheduled. She pointed down a hallway to the Emerald Room.

Nicole opened the door and entered a space whose length was more generous than its width. The side walls appeared to be in sections, part of a moveable partition separating a banquet hall into smaller subdivisions. Two rows of tables and chairs faced each other across an expanse of carpeted flooring. Along the wall by the entrance, another table held coffee and tea urns, plates of muffins and croissants, and a basket of bananas, apples, and grapes.

Nicole was busy adding cream to her coffee when Daniel Leduc, the union business agent, greeted her, his chunky frame stuffed into grey slacks and a light blue, long-sleeve shirt. With much more salt than pepper in his hair and matching beard, he looked like a Santa Claus in waiting.

By the time Leduc's cell phone rang, Alex and Simon had joined them. The call was from Martin Goyette, who was caucusing with other members of the company's negotiating committee in a nearby room. Five minutes later, the management representatives walked in, nodded across at their counterparts, then poured themselves a tea or coffee and sat down at the opposite table. The smiles and pleasantries that had characterized their introductory session in the corporate conference room were absent. Today was all business.

Goyette asked to begin the talks with a discussion of the company's proposals. The union negotiating committee had agreed Leduc would act as spokesman in exchanges with management. He nodded, and a booklet of ten pages was handed to each of them.

"Tanner and Ward must implement major changes as part of a long-term strategy for survival and growth," Goyette said. "Two issues stand out: an obligation to reduce costs and the need for greater flexibility from the workforce. Our proposals are designed to accomplish these goals. Failure to implement them could affect the scope of work and employment at our Montreal site."

The knots in Nicole's stomach tightened, and her heart rate began to ramp up.

"As people retire or leave the company for whatever reason, their positions will be filled by qualified personnel supplied by a third-party contractor responsible for their wages and benefits. These people will not be employees of Tanner and Ward.

"Once we reach the point where they compose fifteen per cent of the workforce, every time a permanent employee leaves, the most senior person working in that occupation for a third-party contractor can apply for the position, and if accepted, will become an employee of Tanner and Ward. This will allow the company to reduce its costs without impacting our current staff."

Nicole grabbed the bottle beside her and drained what remained of the water in two gulps.

Goyette continued. "Two other changes are required. The deductibles paid by current employees for benefits have not kept pace with rising health care costs and must increase from fifteen to thirty per cent. And the defined benefit pension plan has to be converted to a defined contribution plan."

The air conditioning had lowered the room temperature, and Nicole's fingers stiffened as she scribbled down his words. But inside, she was boiling. The concessions being demanded were far more sweeping than anything they had expected. This was a declaration of war.

Goyette had moved on. "Often, due to factors beyond our control, bottlenecks develop in one department, creating a lack of work elsewhere. At those times, personnel must be capable of taking on different tasks outside their usual functions, until the normal workflow can be re-established. For that reason, we're proposing to implement a cross-training program in the shop."

Alex leaned over and whispered in Nicole's ear. "These eejits don't want human beings for employees. They're after a bunch of puppets."

She glanced up and noticed Sophie Martel's gaze was fixed on them, no doubt gauging their reaction.

Goyette concluded by saying that the company would not address any monetary issues until the proposals he'd raised had been dealt with.

In response, Leduc asked for a thirty-minute recess before proceeding. During their caucus meeting, Nicole found herself staring at a vein on the side of Alex's head, which seemed to have come alive. After ten minutes, they calmed down enough to pull together a response everyone agreed with.

When they reconvened, Leduc spoke with passion, his voice rising. He called management's proposals a frontal assault on the rights, income, working conditions, and job security of the employees, and said there would be no agreement on this basis.

He began by insisting they would fight any attempt by management to cut costs by subcontracting permanent jobs and creating a non-union section of the workforce with inferior wages and benefits.

Reverse seniority had to be respected regarding work outside one's occupation based on any cross-training program, and there would need to be a limit on how long such an assignment lasted. The union also demanded that the time period required to reach the top pay rate be reduced from three years to two.

Leduc rejected the company's attempt to make employees pay more for their benefits and reduce its pension obligations, considering the Montreal plant's improved profitability for the third consecutive year. He demanded this prosperity be shared with those who made it possible and proposed a four per cent annual wage increase in a three-year deal, expanded benefits for both employees and retirees, maintenance of the existing pension plan, and stronger language against the contracting out of work.

The colour in Martin Goyette's cheeks deepened as he listened to Leduc. He suggested both parties take a few days to study each other's proposals and meet the following week.

# Chapter 17

The receptionist ushered Alex, Simon, and Nicole into a small meeting room at the regional union headquarters on Côte-Vertu Boulevard. She explained that Daniel Leduc would join them as soon as he wrapped up a call. They settled themselves around the circular table. The dull grey fabric of the steel-frame chairs seemed to match their collective mood. No one appeared very talkative.

They were still coming to grips with yesterday's events. None of them expected what Goyette had laid on the table. His latest monthly email to employees trumpeted the financial turnaround of recent years. That hadn't prepared them for what was coming. Nicole could imagine how people like Annie would react when they heard what management was proposing. But she also knew others would cower in fear of the consequences if they refused the company's demands.

"Sorry for the hold up," Leduc said, as he ambled into the room. The bags under his eyes appeared more pronounced than usual. "How is everyone today?"

"Fuming," Alex said.

Leduc looked at him. "We knew they weren't going to open the vault to us, but I don't think we expected what we heard yesterday. I've sent emails to union representatives at other plants of Tanner and Ward in the UK, Germany, and the U.S. to see if they've faced similar demands. Once these multinationals make a breakthrough at one site, they're quick to try and capitalize on it elsewhere."

"We have to respond right away," Alex said.

"We made our opposition crystal clear yesterday," Leduc replied. "They got the message."

"Maybe they got the message, but they won't change course until they suffer some consequences," Alex countered.

"We can't take any action that affects production until ninety days after the opening of talks," Leduc said. "That's the law. We'll use that time to argue our case and remind them there will be a price to pay if they don't back off."

Nicole turned to him. "There's nothing in the law that says we can't initiate a picket line during our lunch break."

"That's right," chimed in Simon. "We could get people out there for a few minutes, have a brief rally, and be back inside before lunch is over. That would show the company we have the membership behind us."

"You've got what, two, three different lunch periods?" Leduc said. "Getting hundreds of members outside to picket and rally, then back inside in less than thirty minutes won't work. You'll have people coming and going through those turnstiles at the same time. It'll be chaos. You can bet the company will check everyone's clock-out and clock-in times, and anyone who leaves early or returns late will likely be suspended. That will just trigger a backlash against the union, and we'll end up channelling time and resources into fighting the suspensions. We're not going there. We'll do the grunt work of arguing through each other's proposals for the next three months, and then we'll see where we're at."

Nicole and Simon exchanged glances. Alex stared at the table and shook his head. Leduc ignored them. He had already moved on and was flipping through his file folder.

By the time they finished for the day and left the regional office, late afternoon sunshine was poking through gaps in a cloud-streaked sky. On the drive home, Nicole remembered Julie was meeting friends for dinner. That sparked a different thought.

She headed east on the Metropolitan Autoroute, took the exit for L'Acadie Boulevard, and made a left at Jarry. After parking on a side street, she walked in the door, and the co-owner gave her a nod. He gestured towards a table alongside the windows and returned with a pitcher of water and a glass. A menu was stuck under his left arm.

"The usual?" he said.

"Please."

He never handed her the menu because her order never changed. When the heaping silver platter of vegetable biryani was set before her, it took all the discipline she could muster not to wolf it down.

After arriving home, she stretched out on the sofa, savouring her meal, until thoughts of the contract talks resurfaced, and her breathing came in shallow bursts.

## Chapter 18

Between May and August, the members of the union negotiating committee were either locked in debate with the company's representatives at the hotel or huddled together in the small meeting room of the regional office preparing for the next bargaining session. Both sides took a break for two weeks in July, but Nicole was unable to put the negotiations out of mind.

Except for that pause, the same scenario had played out since the talks opened in May. First management presented its demands. Then it was the union's turn. Each presentation produced questions and counterarguments. The company had refused to retreat from any of its positions and claimed the union's proposals were unrealistic.

Nicole was sure management expected them to fold once again at crunch time. But the three of them had agreed not to let that happen. When she checked the scale in the morning, she'd lost two more pounds, and the heavy coffee consumption wasn't doing her sleep patterns any favours.

While Daniel Leduc took the lead in exchanges with company representatives at the bargaining table, Nicole chaired their caucus meetings at the regional office, the latest of which she was trying to wrap up.

"We're approaching the ninety-day deadline," she said. "I think it's time to call on the members. We need more leverage if we're going to push the company back."

"I'm in," Simon said. "It's time for pressure tactics."

Alex nodded in agreement.

"We could meet Thursday and discuss some ideas, then take them to the executive," she suggested.

Leduc looked up from his notes. "I have an arbitration hearing that morning but could join you in the afternoon." He stroked his beard. "Let's see what happens when we meet them tomorrow."

As they packed up, Alex asked if anyone wanted to go for a drink.

Leduc shook his head. "Not me. I still have a few people to phone about the hearing on Thursday."

"Me neither," said Simon. "I've seen more of you than I have of my wife for longer than I can remember, Mac. And nothing personal, but I'd rather look at her than you."

Alex chuckled. "I don't blame you. I scare myself some mornings when I first look in the mirror."

"Only some mornings?" Leduc said.

"Right. So that's two refusals and two insults. Thanks for the love, lads. What about you, Nicole?"

"Annie's dropping by my place, or I'd take you up on the offer. How about a rain check?"

"I'll hold you to that," Alex said.

Nicole phoned Annie from the parking lot at the rear of the building. "We've finished for the day. See you in an hour."

With the union committee either caucusing at the regional office or in bargaining sessions at the hotel, the chance for the two of them to chat at work had been eclipsed by the negotiations.

On reaching home, Nicole noticed breakfast dishes in the sink and began a quick clean up before Annie's arrival. Then she wandered into the living room and stared at the framed photo on the wall, the one with her standing next to Marc as he held

Julie in his arms at the top of the fire tower the weekend they went camping in Vermont.

For the first year after his death, Nicole thought of him daily, and her chest tightened every time that happened. Even now, fifteen years on, whenever she looked at that photo, a wound was reopened.

A high-pitched buzz shattered the silence and made her jump. She hurried to the door.

"Damn," Annie said, "it's been ages." She cradled Nicole's face in her hands. "Just looking for new worry lines. Don't see any, though you're a little dark under the eyes." She took a step back. "Have you lost weight?"

"Don't go there. What will it be? White or red?"

"Let's have something cold," Annie said.

Once Nicole had poured the wine, they moved from the kitchen to the living room. Annie placed her glass on a side table and sank into a chair while Nicole spread out on the sofa.

"So, what's the scuttlebutt?" Annie said.

Nicole watched her swallow a mouthful of wine. "There are some things I can't tell you at the moment. This is a drawn-out process."

"Jeez Louise, I'm not asking for intimate details of your love life. I just want to know what's going on with the talks." Annie took another drink and set down her glass. "People are antsy. Our negotiating team begins meeting with the company, and then poof, it's like you've fallen off the face of the earth. We never see any of you in the shop again." There was an edge to her voice.

"Didn't you get the leaflet explaining we were going through each other's proposals?"

"Yeah, but what did that tell us? Not much. After months of talks, people expect more feedback than that."

"Listen," Nicole said, "there's a chance we'll meet with the executive soon to assess the situation, including the possibility of pressure tactics. But keep that to yourself. Nothing's been decided yet."

Annie studied her for a moment, then drained her drink. "Okay," she said, but her voice lacked conviction.

"More wine?"

Annie handed over her glass.

Nicole retreated to the kitchen, and for the first time, understood how distinct their realities had become. While Annie was stuck on the shop floor wondering what was going on with the talks, she was flitting back and forth between the regional office and the hotel. They were living in different worlds. If she had lost touch with her best friend, what did that mean for the eight hundred others she was supposed to be representing?

# Chapter 19

The union negotiators were in their seats by the time the company's representatives trooped into the meeting room. Goyette opened the session. "We've completed our exchange of proposals, and both parties have had an opportunity to present their arguments," he said. "Based on these discussions, we've prepared an offer to present to the employees."

Nicole recalled Leduc's comment the day before and wondered if he had been tipped off in advance. A copy of the document was handed to each of them.

"Our goal remains to conclude an agreement which is financially responsible for the firm and benefits our workforce long-term," Goyette said. "In addition to the proposals we have made since the opening of these talks, we're offering a two-year contract with increases of two per cent annually to a wage rate which is already highly competitive."

After Goyette finished speaking, Leduc asked for a break so the union side could prepare a response. Once the management representatives had left the room, he turned to the three of them. "Well, what's the verdict?"

"The sooner this is in the bin, the better," Alex said.

"It's the same story every time," Simon added. "The first offer's always a bad joke. Even if they improve it later on, it never comes close to what we need."

Leduc looked at Nicole.

"It's all take and no give," she said. "The company is trying to slash its costs at our expense while making more money every year."

After further discussion, Leduc phoned Goyette, and the company team returned to the room.

"We're of the unanimous opinion that this offer will not be acceptable to our members," he said. "Give us forty-eight hours to prepare a counteroffer."

Goyette stared at Leduc for a moment as if he were considering the proposal. "We've prepared an offer we believe is fair to both parties under the circumstances. Our employees have a right to express their opinion on this, and you have an obligation to give them that opportunity. We want a vote organized as quickly as possible."

There was a moment of silence as his point registered.

Nicole's throat tightened, and it took an effort to speak. "Listen, why waste time and money to vote on something we all know will be rejected? Give us a chance to come back with proposals that can advance the discussion."

Goyette's eyes narrowed. "You listen, Nicole. We can do this the easy way or the hard way. The easy way is for you to organize a vote on this offer. The hard way is for me to contact the Ministry of Labour and demand a meeting be held. Take your pick. Because one way or the other, a vote is going to take place. If I haven't heard from you within twenty-four hours, I will act."

# Chapter 20

The cavernous hall was almost empty. The only occupants were a handful of individuals on afternoon or night shift who had arrived early. In a few minutes, those working days would hop in their vehicles and drive from the plant on Griffith to the hotel on Côte-de-Liesse.

Following Goyette's threat, the union negotiators had decided to proceed with a meeting. At least they couldn't be accused of preventing people from expressing their opinion. And if the result turned out to be what they expected, it would send a strong message. Leduc explained management likely had no illusions this offer would pass but wanted to see how the numbers stacked up. Then the company could calculate what more might be needed to get a settlement.

Goyette expressed his annoyance when Nicole told him it would take a week to organize the vote. Eight hundred copies of the offer had to be printed and distributed to the members by the regional office at least two working days prior to the meeting. This latter provision wasn't a constitutional requirement. It was a practice they had forced the union's regional office to adopt thanks to past battles. People wanted the chance to discuss an offer with their workmates before any vote took place.

From the dais at the front of the room, Nicole watched as floor microphones were set up and the sound system tested.

A bathroom break was in order before the meeting got under way.

Crossing the foyer, she noticed several people having a cigarette outside the doors which opened onto the rear parking lot. That's when she heard her name and spotted Ben Langevin loping towards her.

He was fifty years old, with close-cropped hair and an engaging smile. Three years ago, his wife had left him. For all Nicole knew, maybe for good reason. "She screwed the produce manager of a supermarket," he told her at the time. "Can you believe that? And I thought she spent so much time food shopping cause she liked to cook."

He claimed he'd had his share of opportunities, but unlike his wife, had never cheated. Once he recovered from the shock, it dawned on him he could do more than flirt. But he vowed to shield himself from that kind of hurt again. So now he only looked for casual sex. Their three teenage children stayed with Ben every other weekend. He was always passing around the latest photos. Nicole had seen the kids grow up without ever meeting them.

"Hello princess, long time no see," he said. "What you been up to?"

"Oh, you know, a little gardening, a few day trips here and there. And yourself, Ben?"

"Funny girl. Hey, what's the strongest muscle in the body, relative to size?"

Nicole shook her head.

"The jaw muscle." He tapped the side of his cheek then held up a finger. "One other thing worth knowing. What's a leading medical cause of divorce?"

"I'm sure you're about to tell me," she said.

"Snoring."

"And the point is, Ben?"

"Simple. Today is our chance to exercise those jaw muscles and tell the company negotiators they better stop sawing logs and wake up, or we could be headed for splitsville."

"Thanks for that."

He winked. "Always happy to help."

By the time she returned to her seat on the podium, Daniel Leduc was in conversation with Alex and Simon. Nicole took a drink of water to help settle her stomach. Then, while they waited for people to arrive, she went over the meeting's procedures with the other three.

A rising clamour swept along the outer hallway. Moments later, a river of bodies surged into the room. Long rows of empty chairs were quickly filled. Shouts and greetings escaped from the general commotion as people called to friends and colleagues, indicating empty seats saved for them. Soon the hall was packed, with standing room only along the walls.

Looking out on hundreds of expectant faces, Nicole leaned into the table microphone and tried to keep her voice firm. "Will the stewards please close the doors?"

Conversations ended abruptly, heads turned in her direction, and the crowd became silent.

"We want to begin the meeting."

The words were barely out of her mouth when Robert Simard stepped up to a floor microphone.

"On a point of order."

"Go ahead."

"Why are we voting on something that contains everything the company wants and nothing we asked for? What's our negotiating committee been doing for the past three months?"

His remarks were met with scattered applause.

"Your negotiating committee doesn't like this offer any more than you do," Nicole replied. "When we get to the vote, you'll have a chance to tell the company what you think. But first, let me summarize the main points."

"We don't need a summary," Simard said. "Everyone's read the offer. I move we proceed to the discussion."

The room resounded with a roar of approval.

"All right. Does someone second that motion?"

A forest of arms shot up.

"Those in favour, opposed, carried."

Nicole felt the dampness under her armpits spreading and glanced at her notes. "Please keep your comments brief so that others can speak. I'll indicate when it's time to wind up your remarks. We'll start with microphone one."

Serge Tremblay, an assembler on the Propulsion line, held up a sheet of paper. "I guess everyone's read Goyette's declaration that the financial health of the company depends on it being able to hand over fifteen per cent of the unionized jobs to third-party contractors when our members retire or leave. The workers employed by these outfits get lower wages and fewer benefits than Tanner and Ward's own employees, and this will save the company money. But there's more to it than that.

"Today they want fifteen per cent of the workforce as non-permanent contract workers with fewer rights. Once that's accepted, they'll demand thirty per cent, then fifty per cent. It might take a few years, but sooner or later, the unionized employees could become a minority of the workforce, and you know what that means. Goodbye union. We can't let them head down this road." His remarks ignited a round of applause.

While more than eighty per cent of those in the plant spoke French, a layer of older workers from different nationalities still used English as their primary means of communication. Nicole took notes when people spoke, and if they didn't translate their own remarks, she tried to summarize their

77

comments in the other language so everyone could follow the discussion.

A line of people had begun forming behind each of the microphones set up in the aisles. She pointed toward microphone two. Only ten per cent of the workforce was composed of women, and she knew almost all by name. "Go ahead, Audrey."

"I'm a member of the union pension committee," Audrey Larocque said, "and this is my twentieth year at Tanner and Ward. Nothing personal, but I'd like to avoid spending another two decades with all of you before I can afford to retire."

There was a ripple of laughter.

"The manager in our department said the company wanted to give us more control over the pension fund by changing our defined benefit plan to a defined contribution plan. That's garbage. The company's trying to ditch its responsibility to guarantee our pension when we retire.

"A pension is earned income that's set aside for our retirement. With a defined benefit plan, if the pension fund investments, along with our own annual contributions, don't bring in enough to cover the plan's obligations, the company has to make up the difference and ensure our pension is paid out as promised.

"With a defined contribution plan, the company simply hands over its share and walks away. We're responsible for deciding how to invest the money, and if things don't work out, we could end up at retirement with no pension at all.

"I'm not making this up. One of my uncles lost seventy per cent of his defined contribution pension when the stock market hit the skids in 2008. He was sixty-two years old and never recovered that money before he retired.

"Tanner and Ward first agreed to the defined benefit plan because it was cheap at the time. Thanks to high returns on the invested pension funds and mandatory employee contributions, there were ten years from the 1970s to the 1990s when the company wasn't required to contribute a penny to our pension plan.

"But that's all changed with the current slump. Now, returns on investments are low, and even with employee contributions, there's a growing shortfall the company has to make up. It's trying to avoid those payments and dump its responsibility towards us when we retire. Don't let that happen!"

Her remarks set off a lengthy ovation, and someone shouted, "You tell 'em, Audrey."

Nicole noticed Marcel Bégin at microphone one and gestured towards him.

"I've been here long enough to see some pretty pitiful offers come down the pipes," he said, "but management's outdone itself this time. Did they have a collective wet dream and figure this waste of trees was a contract offer? Only an idiot would vote for this piece of crap."

Laughter and applause broke out as Bégin's fleshy arm sliced the air with the thumb pointing downward.

An older Asian man stood self-consciously at the other microphone.

"Go ahead, Mr. Pang."

As he started to speak, someone shouted, "We can't hear!"

A heavy-set man sitting nearby got up and lowered the microphone.

"Okay now?" Pang asked in English.

"Yeah!" someone yelled.

"I want to know why the company treat us like this?" he said. "We work hard. This is not offer. It is insult!"

Cheers greeted his comment. From the rear of the hall, a chant began to grow. "Insult! Insult! Insult!"

Robert Simard was back at the microphone. "The sentiment of this meeting is obvious," he said. "I propose we end the discussion and move to the vote." More cheers and clapping followed.

"I can't accept that proposal," Nicole said. "You've already spoken, and there are people on the first round still waiting their turn."

Simard made a sweeping motion with his hand as if he were brushing her comment aside and guided the person standing behind him forward.

"I'll make that proposal," the man said.

"And I second it," said the person standing at the other microphone.

"All right, the question's been called. Those in favour of voting on the offer?"

The room was a sea of hands.

"Those opposed?

"The motion is adopted."

Leduc leaned over and whispered in Nicole's ear. She pulled the table microphone closer. "After you vote at the booths set up outside in the hallway, don't leave, because if this is rejected, we'll take a second vote on a strike mandate."

It took an hour to conduct the vote and count the ballots. Nicole showed the results to Leduc, Alex, and Simon, before calling the meeting to order. All eyes were riveted on her. "In favour 37. Against 654. The offer is rejected by 94.6 per cent."

The room erupted. A huge cheer was followed by applause, which took on the character of rhythmic clapping. When the noise died down, Nicole said, "You've told the company what you think of its offer. This next vote will show management what you're prepared to do about it."

Leduc requested the microphone. "We're not proposing you go on strike," he said, "but the company needs to understand your negotiating committee has the authority to act if necessary. Please come back here after you vote to hear the results."

As Nicole stepped down from the stage to join those headed out to vote, someone called her name. Annie leaned in close and whispered, "I haven't been this excited since my last orgasm."

Those on second shift left for work after casting their ballot. The room was two thirds full when Nicole announced a strike mandate of 92.1 per cent, followed by cheers and applause.

Leduc pulled the three of them aside as people filed out. "Martin Goyette asked to be informed of the outcome right away," he said. "I think we should tell him we're available to meet anytime." He turned to Nicole. "Do you want to contact him?"

She dialled his number and explained the results.

"I'll be in touch once we've had a chance to assess the situation," he said and hung up.

After she relayed their exchange to the others, Simon headed home, and Alex went off to the bar in search of Marcel Bégin. Nicole was stuffing papers into her backpack when Leduc asked if she had time for a coffee. He suggested they grab a table in the hotel restaurant where it would be easier to have a chat.

Once they were seated, he said, "What did you think of the meeting?"

"I'm pleased with the vote, but it's usually like that on the first offer."

"You're right," he said. "The real bargaining begins now. Next time we meet them, we'll get a better idea of how determined they are."

"What's your guess?" she said.

He stroked his beard for a moment. "If they don't budge after this vote, we could have a fight on our hands. But let's see how they react next time we meet."

He didn't look optimistic about where this was going. Nicole's lower back clenched, and she shifted in her chair.

Leduc's cell phone rang. He glanced at it, said he should take the call, and sauntered over to an unoccupied corner of the room. As he stared out the window, pressing the phone to his ear, Nicole massaged her back. The waitress had delivered their coffees by the time he returned.

"Sorry about that," Leduc said. "One of my sons wanted to know if he and his buddies could come up to the cottage next weekend for a fishing holiday." He grinned. "I think he's used my new boat more than I have this summer."

After easing himself into his seat, Leduc swallowed a mouthful of coffee and rested his burly forearms on the table. "I've learned a few things about negotiations over the years," he said. "For most of the members, everything's pretty straightforward, either black or white. There's no grey. But the negotiating committee has to examine the situation from different angles, not only what the members want, but also the pressures on the employer. It took me a few years to learn that. It's not necessary to like the people sitting across from us. But sooner or later, we'll have to settle with them."

He took another sip of coffee. "People will be pumped after today's vote. But we've still got some tough bargaining ahead of us. Everyone needs to keep their feet on the ground. Sometimes a few yahoos get carried away and end up trying to drag the membership into a useless confrontation with the employer. Hopefully, we won't have to deal with that here."

He eyed her for a moment, then raised his cup and drained it. His face seemed to relax. "Well, if I hear from Goyette, I'll give you a shout, and you do the same, okay?"

"Sure."

A wall of heat greeted Nicole as she stepped outside the hotel. On the way to her car, she replayed the conversation with Leduc and rotated her head from side to side. Little pops and crackles erupted at the base of her skull. Thanks to the negotiations, she hadn't visited the pool all week. She checked her watch. There was still enough time to go home, grab her suit, and get in an hour of lengths. It was the next best thing to a massage.

# Chapter 21

As she left for work on the first Friday of September, Nicole glanced up at the trees on her street. She knew it wouldn't be long before these leafy green umbrellas in front of her building were speckled with yellow, orange, and red. Every year, she gloried in the changing colours of autumn and tried not to think about the naked branches to follow.

Alex dropped by the union office after his shift and said he'd like to have a chat about the negotiations, so Nicole suggested heading over to a nearby restaurant. Once they were seated, she chose wine, and he asked for a beer. On her return, the waitress took their food order.

They chatted about the recent Quebec election. The defeat of Jean Charest's Liberal government had been due in part to the battle waged by the students against the proposed tuition fee hike. The incoming government was under pressure to cancel it.

"I've talked to a couple of fellas in the shop whose kids were involved in the demonstrations," Alex said. "They're proud of them. Let's hope that fighting spirit rubs off on the parents."

"Well, I can't speak for others," Nicole said, "but it's rubbed off in my household."

The waitress arrived with their food.

While Nicole sampled her salad plate, Alex squirted lemon on his filet of sole and dug in.

"How's the fish?"

"Brilliant."

"So, what did you want to raise with me?"

He finished chewing his food and took a sip of beer.

"You ever hear about the strike at United Aircraft in Longueuil back in the 1970s, Nicole?"

"I've heard mention of it, but don't know the details."

"The company's headquarters were in Connecticut. It was the number one producer of aircraft engines in the world and had never lost a strike at any of its plants." His eyebrows dipped. "The top management in Longueuil was English-speaking and accustomed to throwing its weight around.

"The employees were mainly French-speaking and had a long list of grievances, which included the language of communication but went well beyond that. They were paid less than those at other aerospace plants, faced difficult work schedules, including forced overtime, and had little union security. The place was a tinderbox waiting to blow."

He set down his knife and fork. "The strike dragged on for twenty months, but because of it, the law in Quebec was changed a couple of years later. Every employer was forced to hand over dues from all employees whose wages and working conditions benefitted from representation by a union. We finally caught up with Ontario, where a strike by auto workers won that guarantee thirty years earlier. Quebec's anti-scab law can be traced back to the conflict at United as well. Employers have been working overtime to find ways around it ever since, and often succeeding."

"You're quite the student of labour history, Alex."

"More a participant," he said. "I was working at United Aircraft when the strike happened."

Nicole stopped eating and stared at him.

"United hired a private security firm and gave it free rein against us. There was collusion involving the local cops, the courts, and the company. Right from the start, management rushed out and got injunctions to limit picketing. Scabs hired at government employment centres crossed our lines. Bosses stopped by people's homes and told the men they would lose their jobs if they didn't return to work.

"Those actions just stoked the fire, and the conflict turned increasingly violent. The provincial police targeted militants and tried to recruit informers. While ministers in Bourassa's government tiptoed about, unwilling to take on a powerful multinational company, the international union leadership stabbed the local in the back, accusing it of misusing strike funds.

"Despite the odds stacked against us, we received support from thousands of other workers. They knew that what we were fighting for affected them too. Near the end of the strike, a group of fellas occupied one of the plants. Thirty-four of them were beaten by the riot squad, arrested, and thrown in jail.

"In the end, enough people held together to pull through. When we finally voted to go back, the lads decided to contribute an hour's pay every month to help out the families of those arrested during the occupation of the plant."

"And you were caught up in all that?"

"It was quite a learning experience, for me and many others."

"I can imagine."

"Working to accumulate material things became less important than standing up for something you knew was right. It felt like what you did mattered. How often does that happen in life?"

He picked up his fork and poked at a piece of fish. "Anyway, my point is that leading up to those negotiations, the local leadership established a network to draw in people who wanted to be part of the fight. Many were already active, but others stepped forward as well. I think we need something like that here. From what I see, our steward structure is not built for battle. Some of those guys only drop by the union office to pick up their monthly stipend and flap their gums."

"What would we call this body you're proposing?"

"Call it whatever you like, as long as it's open to anyone who wants to help out."

"I know one person who'd pitch in."

"Who's that?"

"Annie Desjardins. When she came over to my place, it was clear she was frustrated by the slow pace of the talks and wanted to get more involved. I'm sure she's not alone."

The waitress passed by. "How is your meal?"

"Fine, thank you."

"And you, sir?"

"Dead on, thanks."

Nicole watched Alex slice into his baked potato.

"Was United Aircraft the first place you worked when you moved here from Ireland?"

He wiped his lips with a serviette. "It's ironic, you know. My family sent me over here to get away from bombs and guns, and I ended up in the middle of another war. I'm from Belfast, Nicole. The north of Ireland exploded in 1969, and my family was caught up in it. We lived in Percy Street. One night a mob came down our way and attacked all the Catholic homes with petrol bombs. We tried to defend ourselves, but it was no use. Our house was burnt out. I was seventeen years old at the time, and we had to move away."

He stopped talking and took another sip of beer. "You ever hear of Bobby Sands?"

"I don't believe so."

"Aye, you're likely too young to remember. Anyway, I enrolled in technical college to learn a trade, and Bobby was at the same school as me. Both our families had been forced from our homes, and we became friends."

He paused as if lost in the moment.

"In the end, my Da decided to get me out of there. An older sister of his was living in Montreal, so he shipped me over here. United Aircraft was hiring assemblers at the time, and because of my training back home, they took me on a few years before the strike.

"The first weeks after it ended were tough. We found ourselves working alongside people who'd crossed our picket line, and the war zone outside the gates shifted inside. In the end, the union survived, despite an attempt to oust it. Some scabs even became union supporters, thanks to the way they were treated by management following the strike.

"A few months after we returned, I met a couple of fellas in a pub who told me Tanner and Ward was taking people on and suggested I apply. Three weeks later, I got called, did the interviews, and was hired."

"I had no idea you'd been through all that."

He glanced down at his plate. "It was a real roller coaster ride. There were days where you learned more about life in a few hours than all of the preceding year."

"What happened to your school friend in Ireland? Did he move here too?"

Alex looked up, as if surprised by the question. "I'll lend you a book if you'd like. You can read about him. Bobby got involved in resisting the British troops that were sent to the north. He was arrested and died in prison on hunger strike, along with nine other men. They were demanding the British government treat them as political prisoners. Instead, they were called criminals, like the jailed strikers in Longueuil."

# Chapter 22

Fifty people squeezed into a basement meeting room of the Holiday Inn on Côte-de-Liesse. The atmosphere was subdued, the usual joking and banter absent. In addition to the negotiating committee, most shop stewards were present, along with two dozen other members who had stepped forward to join a support committee.

Nicole opened the meeting by explaining they needed a union headquarters off company property. "We found a place on Locke Street, not far from the plant, and the executive decided to sign a short-term lease. We hope matters won't reach the stage of a strike or lockout, but we need to be prepared, just in case."

She turned the floor over to Mike Lafleur, the local's financial secretary. He explained that the first and only work stoppage at the plant occurred in the 1970s. There was no strike pay at the time. By the third week, people couldn't hold out any longer and crawled back for ten cents an hour less than they'd turned down before walking out.

"But one good thing came out of the experience," he said. "A decision was made to set aside money from the monthly membership dues and establish a strike fund for the future. We've built it up to more than $300,000 over the years. That might sound like a lot. But it's only enough to guarantee everyone $150 a week for the first two weeks. Then the national office takes over the payments."

Before opening the discussion period, Nicole mentioned that a leaflet was being prepared for distribution by the support committee to all members in the next few days. "It will urge the company to return to the bargaining table and address the issues raised by the union. If this doesn't happen, the membership will be called on to act."

"What kind of action is being considered?" someone asked.

"We've been discussing a range of tactics that could escalate over time. If you have any suggestions, now's the time to raise them."

That kicked off a lively exchange lasting an hour.

As the meeting wound up, Nicole felt better than she had in ages. Until now, the pressure to succeed in these talks had rested on the shoulders of the negotiating committee. With the launching of a support committee, others had stepped forward to help, including Annie.

She pulled Nicole tight against her hip and grinned. "Sisters in struggle once again."

Nicole put an arm around her friend's waist. "How long has it been? Almost twenty years?"

"Did you have to mention that?" Annie muttered. "Now you've ruined the moment, just when I was starting to feel young and vibrant again."

# Chapter 23

The rhythmic clicking in the hallway grew louder, and Martin Goyette glanced up from the papers spread out before him. Sophie Martel swept through the doorway of the corporate conference room in a light grey suit, her shoulder-length hair swaying from side to side with each step.

"Good afternoon, Sophie. I hope you're finding the experience on the negotiating committee a useful one."

She smiled back at him. "Yes, it's been a good crash course in learning about the business. Thank you for agreeing to include me."

"No need to thank me. It was your suggestion. We just embraced an innovative idea which should accelerate your integration into the team here at Tanner and Ward."

Goyette appreciated the energy and enthusiasm she brought to the committee. As a relative newcomer to the management team, her questions and observations provided a fresh perspective. She was a quick learner, articulate, and able to defend her point of view. Goyette thought she had a chance to rise in a company that was always on the look-out for new talent to deploy across its international network. Being a woman could even work in her favour. The firm was eager to diversify its image without diluting the quality of leadership required in an increasingly competitive world.

As other members of the committee arrived, Goyette welcomed each one in turn, then opened the meeting.

"The proposals we've made in these negotiations are based on consultations with the executive committee in London under Sir Edmund's leadership. The need to achieve our goals represents a major challenge for us as a management team. How well we do in this regard will influence company decisions about where to assign future work.

"If something can be handled more cost-efficiently elsewhere, that's where it will go. We will not receive new engine lines, component repair orders, or investment, and could even lose work we presently do. We not only have to be cost-competitive with other companies in the marketplace, but also with other sites of Tanner and Ward in the Americas, Europe, the Middle East, and Asia."

Goyette paused and settled back in his chair. "There is a second element to consider regarding these negotiations," he said. "Eight years ago, we were given a mandate by the UK to develop an industrial version of the Hermes aircraft engine. One of these can produce up to fifty megawatts of power. That's enough electrical output for as many as fifty thousand homes. With growing global concern over future energy sources, there is enormous potential for this type of product.

"We're in a race with two of our main competitors who are developing similar engines. The first one to comply with safety and environmental standards and get their brand on the market could reap significant financial rewards. We want to be the one. Our engineers tell us we're close to achieving this. The only remaining challenge is reducing the emission of certain gases to meet environmental guidelines. We're working flat out to solve that problem."

Goyette placed his forearms on the table. "The challenge before us is to achieve the cost reduction goals proposed by Sir Edmund and his team, and that will require some tough bargaining on our part. At the same time, we want to avoid an interruption in production at this facility because of the point we're at in the development of the industrial Hermes engine.

"To bring these negotiations to a successful conclusion, I'm proposing we convene a series of meetings with the shop floor employees where we can explain why our proposals must be implemented to secure their jobs and the future of this site. After that, we can resume talks with the union."

## Chapter 24

Martin Goyette walked into the meeting room, where he was greeted by Paul Dufour. To his left, several dozen employees were seated on folding chairs.

"I've set up the laptop, and everything is ready for your presentation," Dufour told him. "Perhaps we should wait a few more minutes to make sure everyone's arrived."

Dufour's presence was a bonus. While there were those in the room who might harbour a grudge, Goyette was sure others still respected the man who had served as their union president for a decade. His participation could help sway some of those in attendance.

After placing his notes on the front table, Goyette noticed a familiar face and walked over to the first row of employees. "Good morning, Karl. Did you watch the Singapore Grand Prix on Sunday?"

"Yes, Martin, I did. Even though the race ended with a couple of laps remaining because of the two-hour limit, I'm pleased Vettel won."

Goyette nodded. "I'm already looking forward to next year's Formula One race here," he said. "I was out of the country on business in June and missed it, the first time in years. Did you go?"

"No. I wasn't able to," the man said. "My wife's sister and her family were in town that weekend."

As they chatted, Dufour approached. "I think we can begin whenever you're ready."

Goyette thanked him and turned back to Karl. "Maybe you'll win next year's draw for company tickets, and we can watch the race together."

"That would be great," he said.

Paul Dufour opened the meeting. "Thank you for being here. Mr Goyette will speak, and then there will be time for questions."

Goyette surveyed his audience to ensure he had everyone's undivided attention. "As you know, the company and the union are currently engaged in talks to reach agreement on a new contract. I thought it would be worthwhile to explain why we're proposing certain changes.

"We operate in a very competitive industry. The executive committee of Tanner and Ward in London has instructed all sites worldwide to lower costs in order to retain current customers and win new ones. Otherwise, work will go elsewhere, and staffing levels will drop. This isn't a threat," he said. "These are simply facts."

Goyette knew this wasn't what his audience wanted to hear, and it frightened them. He nodded at Paul Dufour, who was seated next to the laptop. A graph appeared on the screen behind him.

"The changes required here include replacing up to fifteen per cent of current employees who retire or leave the company with qualified workers provided by a third party. These people would not be employees of Tanner and Ward, though they could become so when such positions open up. This will allow the company to reduce its costs and will not affect any of you.

"We also need greater flexibility to boost productivity, an increased contribution by employees to sustain current benefits, and a revision of the pension plan. In implementing these measures, our goal remains to provide the maximum number of positions with the best wages, benefits, and working conditions possible, based on market conditions."

More slides followed, demonstrating the need for each of these changes. The final one flashed the masthead of a local daily across the screen with the headline, "Tanner and Ward closes its doors after 60 years in Montreal."

Goyette lowered his voice. "None of us want to see this. By reaching agreement in these negotiations, we can ensure it doesn't happen." Sober faces stared back at him. After a moment, the screen went blank. He turned to the table behind him and took a sip of bottled water.

"Any questions?"

A woman with a ponytail raised her hand. "Go ahead," he said.

"Why are we being asked to give up more when the company's doing better every year?"

Goyette began pacing back and forth. "If we don't make the adjustments I've outlined, the progress here won't continue, and that will have serious consequences for us all." He turned and faced his audience.

"Let me give you an example. For the company to operate efficiently, our workforce needs to be matched with our workload. The new cross-training program Paul is heading up will make this possible, because every employee will be trained to carry out at least two different tasks, their primary job and a secondary one.

"Despite our best efforts, factors beyond our control mean that priorities can switch at short notice, and bottlenecks develop in one area which reduce the workload elsewhere. When that happens, we need to switch some people from their usual job to the priority task and re-establish the required workflow. Who moves where will depend on the skills needed, and we will ensure people receive the proper training."

A slim man with horn-rimmed glasses raised his hand. "Just on your last point," he said. "This cross-training program you're pushing means we can be bounced around from job to job at the whim of management and forced to work outside our usual occupation for who knows how long. I don't like it, and I'll tell you why.

"When you start here, you don't have enough seniority to work steady days and are forced to rotate shifts every month. This can go on for years. If it causes too many family problems, you try to avoid rotating shifts by volunteering for straight evenings or midnight shift. Working those hours isn't the best way to connect with your children or spend time with your spouse. It also helps account for the divorce rate and the dependency problems some people are dealing with here.

"As the most junior employee, you have last choice for vacation, and it can take up to a decade before you get holidays in the summer when your kids are off school and your wife's not working. If there's a layoff, you're the first to go and the last called back.

"After fifteen or twenty years, things improve. You have enough seniority to work steady day shift. You get your vacation in the summer with your family and have less chance of being laid off when there's a downturn in work."

The man's voice had risen, and he pointed a finger in Goyette's direction. "Now you want the right to decide who is trained for what secondary tasks, when they're assigned to them, and for how long. If I happen to be conversant on a secondary job where there are often bottlenecks, I can be shifted around frequently. Meanwhile, a newer employee who has been trained for a task where there's rarely an overload of work remains in the department.

"The little bit of stability I've been able to establish in my life disappears. We're back to a situation where management can treat people arbitrarily, and fairness goes out the window. If this approach is implemented in your cross-training program, what's next? Shifts? Vacations? Layoffs? Where does it end?"

As he sat down, applause erupted from several parts of the room. Goyette removed his jacket and laid it across the table next to the laptop. "How long have you worked here?" he asked.

"Twenty-three years," the man said.

"I'm sure you've seen quite a few changes during that time, various shifts, new engine lines, different work rules and procedures. That's just the nature of our business. Nothing is static. If we want to survive and grow, we must change and adapt. The market dictates those changes, and we must respond. I appreciate your concerns and know what it means not to spend time with your family. I don't have a choice about going to the UK every couple of months for meetings that include weekends.

"We all have to focus on the big picture. If we're asked to make sacrifices, it's to protect what matters most—secure employment with good working conditions, wages, and benefits. These are what enable us to provide for our families and enjoy the time we have with them. The changes we're proposing are needed to maintain all of this."

Goyette planted his feet and put his hands on his hips. "There can be no sacred cows. We need to be innovative and do whatever it takes to show our customers we can meet their needs better than anyone else. I'm convinced we can rise to the challenge. If I didn't believe that, I wouldn't be standing here. I have faith in you, and I'm confident we can agree on the changes needed."

An older worker at the back of the room raised his hand, and Goyette gestured towards him. The man rose from his chair. He was tall, with slightly stooped shoulders.

"Just a quick comment," he said. "From my vantage point, it looks like all the sacrifices are coming from one side. You're asking us to pay twice as much to maintain our benefits without any improvement in them, while you dump your obligations to our current pension plan. Now you want to start a cross-training program that will give management new ways to discriminate, and we know it won't end there. That doesn't look like equal sacrifice to me. It sounds like your power to call the shots increases, and we take a financial beating."

His remarks drew more applause.

"And by the way," he added, "being away from your family over the weekend because you're flying first-class to London and staying in a five-star hotel, is not the same as being forced in on mandatory overtime to rebuild an engine in thirty-degree heat with sweat pouring off you because management says it's too expensive to air-condition the plant, though not the offices, including yours."

Laughter erupted across the room.

Goyette took a deep breath and exhaled slowly. He wouldn't allow himself to be goaded. Instead, he lowered his voice once again. "You're welcome to your opinion," he said, "though if you were to accompany me to those meetings overseas, you'd see it's not the bed of roses you make it out to be. There's a great deal of responsibility involved, and it's hard work, maybe not physically, but mentally and emotionally. It can be very draining when you're responsible for the welfare of hundreds of people and their families. In any event, I'm not complaining. I enjoy the challenge.

"We can't have this attitude that management and employees are adversaries. We're not. We're on the same team, striving for the same thing, which is to make this company as successful as possible and all share in that success. We can never lose sight of our common interests."

The man had remained standing. "I was hired here twenty-eight years ago because I needed a job to survive, and this company needed workers like me. If you want to talk about common interests, that's where they started, and that's where they ended.

"This company is not in business to provide good-paying jobs to people like me," he said. "It's in business to make money, which means maximizing productivity and minimizing costs. Our wages, benefits, and pension are a major cost which the company tries to limit as much as possible. So there's a conflict of interest between what management wants and what we need. If you don't believe me, look at what happens every time we renegotiate our contract. We always have disagreements over how much of the revenue produced by our labour comes back to us, and what portion is scooped up by the company."

This time he sat down.

"It's true that management and employees don't always see eye to eye," Goyette said. "But is this because we have conflicting interests or due to a lack of understanding of our common interests? You say it's the former. I would argue it's the latter.

"If the cost of employees' wages and benefits makes a company no longer competitive, and it loses customers, who suffers? Everyone. Employees, management, and the shareholders. We can't approach this in terms of separate interests. That only undermines our collective interests, and when that happens, who wins? Our competitors. And if they win, we all lose."

The man rose from his chair again. When he spoke, there was no disguising the anger. "According to your logic, employees should welcome anything the company says will make it more competitive, even if that's at our expense. We're not as dumb as you seem to think. Your push for greater flexibility and cross-training has nothing to do with increasing our job security. Exactly the opposite. The goal is to slash the workforce and cut costs. And once you start replacing permanent employees with cheaper workers provided by a contractor, it's only a matter of time until you come after the rest of us and try to get rid of the union."

"Your disagreement is not with management," Goyette countered. "It's with the market. I'm just telling you what's required if we're to survive in today's competitive conditions. You're free to reject my advice. But be prepared for the consequences. The future of this company and your own future are in your hands."

He stopped speaking and scanned the crowd. Some people were gazing at the floor, but most were staring back at him. Behind the sombre faces, he knew the gears were turning.

"If there are no further questions, I'll let you get back to your departments. Thank you for coming. With your understanding and assistance, I'm confident we can look forward to a successful resolution of these talks."

## Chapter 25

During the last two weeks of September, Martin Goyette addressed all shop floor employees in a series of departmental meetings designed to shift opinion in favour of management's proposals. The union responded by having the support committee distribute a leaflet explaining the scope of the company's attack on the employees' income, rights, and working conditions despite increased profits. When talks resumed, another round of discussion on the demands of both sides produced no change.

The next day, members of the support committee were summoned to the union office, where Nicole explained the talks had stalled. "Tell everyone in your department that following the Thanksgiving weekend, no overtime is to be worked by union members." When someone asked how long this would last, she answered, "as long as necessary."

Nicole knew the boycott would not be popular with those who had come to rely on voluntary overtime and factored it into their income as a permanent feature. To enforce the ban, the union organized teams at both entrances the first day it was to take effect.

Nicole pulled into the rear parking lot at three fifteen in the morning and made her way to the turnstiles leading into the plant. She was greeted by Mike Lafleur, the union's financial secretary, who was sipping coffee and shifting his weight from one foot to the other. They chatted in the chilly early morning hours and were soon joined by Annie and Simon.

The parked cars of those working midnight shift were scattered across the lot. Only the muffled sound of the odd transport truck rumbling by on Griffith Street at the front of the building disturbed the silence. Nicole gazed through the chain-link fence and noticed that the roller door at the rear of the plant was closed, the one through which engines wrapped in plastic covers and cradled in metal stands were shuttled in and out on the forks of large lift trucks. All was quiet at the moment. But today was a test. To what extent would the union's appeal be respected?

A beam of light sliced through the darkness, and a vehicle pulled into the lot. Lamp posts illuminated several footpaths that converged on the turnstiles at the rear of the plant. Inky patches separated the lighted walkways. They heard a car door slam and waited to see who emerged from the shadows.

A tall figure carrying a backpack over one shoulder appeared between two rows of cars. The loping walk looked familiar, but before Nicole could speak, Simon said, "It's Ben Langevin."

When Ben saw them, he waved. "Well, the gang's all here."

Nicole's throat tightened, and she had to force the words out. "You're early, Ben."

"We have a few knuckleheads in my department who might want to work overtime, so I figured I'd see who showed up and make sure everybody knew about it."

Her shoulders relaxed. "You had us worried for a minute. We thought you might be heading in yourself."

Langevin's eyes widened. "Are you crazy? Goyette's been on our backs for years. Now we're finally standing up and doing something. I'm ready for action."

Simon extended his hand. "Glad to have you as part of the welcoming committee. Remember, our goal is explanation, not intimidation. If we can't convince someone not to do overtime, we won't try and physically stop them. That will just lead to problems."

"Don't worry," Ben said, "there'll be no need for rough stuff. Anyone doing overtime will have a lot of visitors at their workstation in the course of the day. I don't think they'll want to repeat the experience."

He slid the backpack off his shoulder and pulled out a thermos. "I came prepared," he said.

They watched him take a swig.

"Is that coffee or something stronger?" Annie asked.

"Ah, that's for me to know, and you to find out, my dear." Ben puckered up his lips and stuck out his chin.

"Fat chance!" she said. "Whatever's in that thermos is between you and it. I'm not getting involved."

"Smart girl," Ben replied. "Hey, you know how many bacteria are transferred in a ten-second kiss?" No one spoke. "Eighty million. Kinda puts smooching in a different light, doesn't it?"

Annie rolled her eyes.

Headlights swept across the entrance to the parking lot, and a vehicle disappeared behind a row of cars. They heard a door close and soon noticed a figure walking slowly towards them.

Ben was the first to recognize Denis Leclair. "Our number one grabber. Never miss a chance to do some overtime, eh Denis?"

"Hey, what's up?" Leclair said.

Nicole stepped towards him. "Morning, Denis. The union is asking our members not to work overtime. We need the company to back off its demands and begin addressing our issues. That won't happen unless we cut into its revenue."

"How long will that take?"

"We don't know, but we all have to stick together on this. It's for everyone's benefit."

Leclair glanced at his watch. "So what'll I do for the next three hours?"

"You're welcome to stay with us."

He looked at her with a blank expression. "Well, I was going to change the oil in my wife's car after work. Guess I can head home and do it now. Hope this gets settled soon. I've got my own revenue to worry about."

"Denis, you've been here long enough to know things can happen during negotiations," Ben said. "You should always put some money aside in advance. What would you do if the company locked you out tomorrow?"

Leclair scowled at Ben. "Not all of us are rich like you, Langevin."

"Yeah, right," Ben said. "Put that heap of junk I drive next to your car, and we'll see who has money to burn. Look at it this way, Denis. If you're not getting up early to do overtime, that means more beauty rest. And lord knows you could use it."

Nicole raised her open hand towards Ben. "Thanks for respecting the boycott, Denis. We want this settled as quickly as possible."

"Yeah, let's hope so." He glared at Langevin, then swung around and headed to his car.

Once Leclair was out of earshot, Ben said, "That's the kind of knucklehead I mentioned earlier."

Nicole turned on him, and her voice rose a notch. "Listen. We're not here to antagonize people. We're trying to win them over. Insulting them doesn't help."

Ben's smile faded. He glanced down at his feet for a moment, then back at her. "Yeah, okay."

Aside from Leclair, only four others showed up for overtime. A similar number arrived at the front entrance, where they were greeted by another team. After a discussion, each person agreed not to go in. By the end of the day, the boycott was in place.

# Chapter 26

The overtime ban had been respected all week despite grumbling from some quarters. Meanwhile, the company appeared in no rush to re-start the stalled talks. Work was proceeding as usual on the regular shifts, and engines were leaving the shop, though deliveries would soon begin falling behind schedule without overtime.

Would management stop inducting engines and divert them to other company sites? That had happened in the past when offers were rejected or pressure tactics applied. Such a move could spark fear of layoffs or a lockout and pave the way for acceptance of the latest proposals.

Mike Lafleur was hunched over a desk in the union office working on the monthly budget when Nicole told him she was leaving for half an hour and to call her if anything urgent came up. After bumping into Annie in the locker room, she had agreed to meet her for lunch in the cafeteria. Before Nicole made it that far, Marcel Bégin motioned her over as she passed by the machine shop.

"Hi, Marcel. How's it going?"

He removed his earplugs. "No one is doing overtime, and the foremen are going through the roof. They're asking guys for reasons when they refuse, and they're threatening them, saying if the overtime isn't done, the company will lose customers, and there'll be layoffs in the department.

"Besides that, anyone who scraps a part is being disciplined. This morning they suspended a young guy who was working on a new machine for the first time. He shaved an extra twelve one-thousandths of an inch off a casing. Okay, it was a mistake, and the part was scrapped, but they've got to expect that with their goddam cross-training program."

"Who's the foreman?"

"Gilbert Larose."

"You want to come with me? We'll go see him now."

Larose was seated at his desk in the foreman's office, a cubicle of shoulder-high walls at the rear of the machine shop. He turned as Nicole approached and looked up over his glasses. "Yes ma'am, what can I do for you?"

"Gilbert, I understand some people have been refusing overtime, and they've been hearing about it from the foremen."

"Not some people, Nicole. Everyone is refusing overtime. Five engines need to be out of here in the next week, or the company's going to be paying a hefty penalty for late delivery. To get them out, we'll have to drop other jobs, and by this time next week, we'll be even further behind schedule."

"You have no right to ask people for reasons if they refuse overtime," she said. "It's voluntary unless you use clause twenty-nine point two and force them in for their eight hours a month. And I understand you're suspending people for any scrapped part, even if it's during the cross-training program. I'm telling you, Gilbert, the union will fight every single suspension, and based on past practice, we'll have a strong chance of winning most of those cases. In the meantime, you'll have fewer machinists available to do the work."

"Don't tell me how to run this department," he barked. "And you better think about what you're going to say to your members if we lose business and people get laid off, cause it'll be the union's fault."

"I'm not telling you how to run your department, and you don't tell me how to do my job. Just follow the collective agreement and stop hassling the guys."

Larose glared at them, then with a dismissive wave, returned to the paperwork on his desk.

As they walked back to Marcel's machine, he turned to Nicole. "I've never seen you like that before."

Her thumping heart and parched throat made speaking an effort. "Sorry, I lost it there for a minute."

"No, it was good," he said.

After reaching the cafeteria, she headed for the fountain and gulped down a mouthful of water, then surveyed the room. Annie was soaking up the last of the spaghetti sauce on her plate with a piece of bun and looked up as Nicole approached.

"What took you so long?" she said. "Is the Alzheimer's kicking in early? I'm due back at my workstation in fifteen minutes."

"Blame your sick sense of humour," Nicole countered. "I wasn't sure I could take it for a full half-hour."

That brought a smile to Annie's face.

## Chapter 27

Nicole was busy slicing tomatoes for a salad when Julie came home from class.

"Hi, honey. Ready to eat in a few minutes?"

"Yeah, Mom. I'll just wash up and give you a hand."

On her return, she asked if there was any news about the negotiations.

"We're trying to apply more pressure, but so far, there's been no movement on their part. If the situation escalates, you may be preparing some dinners on your own."

"It's already rare enough to have a meal with you," Julie said.

"How was your day?" Nicole asked.

"Depressing."

"How so?"

"I saw this young guy sitting on the floor in the Metro station holding a handmade sign asking for money to eat. He was in rough shape—scraggly hair, dirty clothes, torn sneakers. I felt so bad, seeing him like that. He was staring at the floor with this hopeless look on his face. I put some change in the empty coffee cup beside him, and he didn't even glance up. Obviously, he needs more help than just food money. I see so many people like him every day."

Julie removed a second cutting board from the wall and placed it on the counter. "I remember reading a news story last month about somebody who recovered from a situation like that, but how many never do? What happens to them?

We're just supposed to go on with our lives as if it doesn't matter?"

Nicole stopped slicing the tomatoes and set down her knife. "I'm proud of you."

"For giving the guy some coins?"

"For feeling the way you do, for caring."

"So, what can be done?" Julie said.

"Well, I guess if enough people get together and try to do something, that might make a difference."

"But where do you start?"

"If you feel like this, there must be others who think the same way. You just have to find each other."

Julie looked at her mother as if she were giving this some thought. "Yeah, I guess so." She opened a drawer, took out a knife, and began slicing a cucumber for the salad.

## Chapter 28

All morning Nicole had been answering calls from members who had heard from so and so of a conversation between someone else and a foreman who reportedly said that because of the overtime boycott the company had no choice but to stop inducting engines which would lead to layoffs. Was the negotiating committee aware of this? Was it meeting with the company? Was there a new offer?

Her efforts to reach Martin Goyette for clarification received no response. By early afternoon, Nicole was on her third coffee of the day and struggling to hide the fact that she was a soggy mass of jitters. Shortly before three o'clock, he returned her call and confirmed a negotiating session at the hotel the following day.

Goyette nodded across at the union negotiators as he led the management team into the meeting room just after nine in the morning. Once they had settled themselves, he opened the discussion.

"Because of your decision to organize a boycott of overtime, we have no alternative but to stop inductions. We can't take the chance of having our customers' engines tied up in a labour dispute. This will have repercussions for the employees. As work dwindles, we will be forced to implement layoffs. We sincerely regret the need for such action but have no other choice.

"For our part, we want to find a way out of this impasse. In the interest of reaching a just and equitable settlement, we have prepared a new and final offer which includes two major changes. We will double the company's contribution to the pension of each employee for the next two years if the plan is changed. And we will grant a $2,000 signing bonus if the offer is accepted."

Copies of the proposal were passed across to members of the union committee.

"These are significant monetary improvements," Goyette said. "At the same time, if all the other elements of the offer are implemented, we can reduce our operating costs as required. It will be a win-win for the company and its employees."

"No, it won't," Nicole blurted out. "You're just trying to buy people off as cheaply as possible." She noticed Daniel Leduc's head snap in her direction.

Goyette blinked, and the corner of his mouth twitched. "Listen, Nicole. This is more than a fair offer in today's market conditions."

"No, it's not. The signing bonus you offer is a one-time pay-ment. It won't be rolled into long-term wage increases or pension benefits. And tell me how doubling your contribution for two years to a pension that may not even be there at retirement, is an improvement over one that's more likely to be available when we need it?

"You're making good money here, thanks to the efforts of our members. But instead of recognizing this, you want to increase your control over our lives, force more concessions on us, stick a bow on that, and call it a fair and final offer. We understand the difference between negotiation and ultimatum. And don't think everyone isn't aware of the perks upper manage-ment gets—the company cars, the stock options, the year-end bonuses, the promotions. People are fed up with having to scratch and claw every time we negotiate, just to hold on to what's necessary and gain what's needed."

Narrowed eyes and clenched jaws replaced the usual smug expressions at the opposite table.

"We'll need time to consider these changes and get back to you," Leduc said sharply.

Goyette nodded. The management team rose and left the room.

Leduc sprang up from his chair, marched over to the opposite table, and hoisted himself up on it, so he was facing the three of them. Then he slammed his notebook down.

"Just what the fuck was that?" he said.

No one spoke.

"Didn't we agree on no off the cuff remarks? We caucus first and then present our response. That way, we don't lock ourselves into positions we might want to change later. I thought we were clear on this." He wiped the back of his hand across his mouth.

Nicole lowered her gaze and rolled a pen between her thumb and index finger. She knew she'd lost it there. This wasn't like her. Or was it? Didn't the same thing happen with the machine shop foreman? Before she slid further down a dark hole, Alex spoke.

"I have no problem with what Nicole said."

"She only told them what they needed to hear," Simon added.

Leduc tugged at his beard. "I'm not saying I disagree with what she said. But we should never react on the spot. If we don't come back with the opinions Nicole expressed, they know we have internal differences. And that doesn't strengthen our bargaining hand."

Nicole bit her lower lip. "Sorry for not holding my tongue."

Leduc eyed her for a moment. He pushed himself off the table and walked behind it, then yanked out a chair and sat down. "All right, let's move on."

Everyone decompressed.

Leduc tugged at his beard again. "Any further thoughts on the offer?"

"What's changed since the opening day of negotiations?" Alex said. "Almost all their original demands are still there. But do you see any of our proposals?"

"Exactly," said Simon. "We spend all our time trying to block the concessions they want, while the improvements we propose are brushed aside."

Leduc wrote down their comments in his notebook. He glanced over at Nicole. "You have anything to add?"

She shook her head. "I've said my piece."

Leduc removed his glasses and rubbed his eyes. "Companies are pushing hard to change how matters were handled in the past. And the reason given is always the same—to be more competitive. The world is a smaller place for them. What they gain at one site they want everywhere, and if they don't get it, they threaten to move the work.

"According to Tanner and Ward's annual report, they recently hired two hundred engineers in India to work on the research and development of a new engine. This is the first facility they've opened there. They got tax and land concessions and cherry-picked the best and brightest minds at a fraction of the cost of doing this work in Europe or North America. Give them time to figure out how to cut their supply-chain costs, and they'll build a production facility there as well.

"I know we still have leverage here in Montreal thanks to the test beds, an experienced workforce, the exchange rate, tax breaks, and government subsidies. But conditions change. They're serious about cutting costs by squeezing more production from fewer people. We need to look ahead ten or fifteen years and negotiate agreements that protect jobs in the long term."

No one spoke.

Nicole finally broke the silence. "None of us can say for sure what conditions will be like in ten or fifteen years. But it's a safe bet we'll still have to fight for what we need, and nothing will be handed to us. In the meantime, we've got to deal with their offer, and I can't recommend it."

Simon leaned forward and clasped his hands in front of him. "I'm with Nicole," he said.

Alex nodded in agreement.

"Okay," Leduc replied, "you three are the negotiating committee, and if you can't recommend this offer, that's the way it is. But if you propose rejection, and we end up with layoffs, people are going to blame you, because the company warned that's what would happen."

He stroked the top of his head. "This may be far from the deal we'd like. But is it the best we can get in the circumstances? Don't let your members off the hook and set yourselves up to be accused of sacrificing their jobs. You don't have to propose rejection or acceptance. You can simply present the offer without a recommendation and let people make up their own minds."

In the end, the three of them accepted Leduc's proposal. Despite concern about abdicating their responsibility to express an opinion on the offer, they agreed it was the members' right to choose.

# Chapter 29

Nicole took her seat on the dais at the front of the vast hall and poured herself a glass of water. The cold liquid slid down easily but failed to settle her stomach. Today's meeting promised to be livelier than the previous one. The nearly unanimous rejection of a first offer could seem like a distant memory if opinion shifted dramatically in the opposite direction. It all depended on what proposals the company made and how confident or threatened people felt.

Over the years, Nicole had heard committee recommendations denounced as sellouts or praised as victories, seen screaming matches between members with opposing views, and witnessed euphoric cheering after offers were voted up or down.

While talks were in progress, rumours circulated on the shop floor. There was a strict policy that bound negotiating committee members not to disclose any information about an offer before its distribution to the membership. Despite that, private conversations with relatives or friends leaked out, fuelling speculation.

Once an offer was printed and distributed across the plant, the discussion was joined. Opinions formed, debates broke out, and positions hardened. Word spread that the guys in the test beds were against it while those in the machine shop were split. A majority on the Propulsion line favoured it, but most on the T24 line were opposed. Some people organized pools. Whoever came closest to the actual result took home the cash. The only guaranteed winner was the hotel bar. It always did a brisk business after the meeting, regardless of the outcome.

At three o'clock, Nicole asked the stewards to usher everybody inside and close the doors. The noise in the room ebbed away. Flanked by Alex, Simon, and Leduc, she looked out once again at hundreds of expectant faces.

Nicole began by presenting a brief summary of the offer. She asked people to limit their remarks, so everybody who wanted to speak could do so, then pointed to microphone number one. "Go ahead, brother."

A young man introduced himself as Patrick and said he worked on the T24 line. "There's been a lot of discussion the past few days in my department regarding this offer. Some people don't like it and want to vote it down. Others aren't sure we can get anything better. There's also fear of a layoff if we say no. I'd like to hear what the negotiating committee thinks about all this."

Nicole swallowed hard. "You've had a chance to read what the company gave us at the bargaining table. In response to our rejection of the first offer and the ban on overtime, management is proposing to double its pension contribution for the next two years if the plan is changed and throw in a $2,000 signing bonus. Is this movement enough? That's for you to decide. The only thing I can add is that we were told if this offer was rejected, there would be layoffs. We don't know whether management's bluffing or how many people would be affected."

Suddenly the room was abuzz. Everyone seemed to be talking at once. A line of speakers had formed behind Patrick, and another was taking shape at the second microphone.

"So what do you, as our negotiating committee, think we should do?" he asked.

Nicole took another sip of water. The chatter on the floor had dried up, and all eyes were on her. "We're making no recommendation one way or the other. We don't like the company's offer because it contains everything management wants and nothing we've asked for, but we can't ignore the threat of layoffs. It's for you to decide. Whatever that decision is, we'll act on it."

She pointed to the other side of the room. "Microphone number two."

A tall young man with long brown hair leaned down to speak. "I've only worked here for a year and a half," he said, "and I understand why people don't like this offer. But if we say no, I'm probably one of the people who'll be let go. Just look around. Maybe wages and benefits are better at some other companies, but we're not so bad off compared to lots of other places. That's all I wanted to say."

There was a smattering of applause from two rows of younger workers nearby.

Donny Taylor, who had chaired the union committee responsible for organizing the presidential election, stepped up to the microphone. He lived in Kahnawà:ke, a First Nations community on the shore of the St. Lawrence River, south of Montreal. Mohawks there blockaded the nearby Mercier Bridge in the summer of 1990 during what became known as the Oka crisis. The action was in solidarity with their kin in Kanehsatà:ke, sixty kilometres to the northwest, who were under siege for erecting a barricade to stop the expansion of a golf course and the building of condominiums on their ancestral lands.

Taylor stood with his people and did not report to work during the blockade of the bridge, which lasted seven weeks. After using up what remained of his holidays, he was phoned by his foreman who threatened him with dismissal unless he returned to work. Taylor contacted his shop steward. In response, a meeting was arranged with management, which finally agreed no Mohawk employees would be disciplined for their absence during a political crisis they were not personally responsible for. Following his return, Taylor became active in the union.

"I'd like to tell the brother who spoke before me that none of us want to see him or anyone else here lose their job. This isn't the first time the company has tried to blackmail us into accepting an offer with the threat of layoffs."

"It's not a threat," someone yelled. "It's going to happen if we vote no."

Taylor looked in the direction of the voice. "No one wins if we accept this deal except the company. We'll all lose on job security, wages, benefits, and our pension. Thanks to their cross-training program, they'll be able to jerk us around from job to job at a moment's notice. And once they start replacing permanent employees with cheaper contract workers, the door is open to wiping out the union. It's time to stand up and say no."

His remarks received a solid ovation.

"I just want to add one thing," he said. "I'm disappointed with our committee. We elected you to lead us in these negotiations, and you have a responsibility to tell us what you think. In answer to Patrick's question, Nicole explained the committee doesn't like this offer. Then why didn't you recommend rejection? We may or may not agree with your proposal, but we have a right to know your opinion, and you have a responsibility to tell us."

Before Nicole could respond, Leduc asked for the microphone.

"Brother, as business agent, I suggested the negotiating committee not make a recommendation on this offer. Let me explain why. If it proposes voting no, after the company has threatened layoffs, and then people lose their jobs, who are those people going to blame? Not the company. They know it's responsible for throwing them out of work. But they'll feel the negotiating committee betrayed them because it recommended rejecting the offer.

"The members of your committee have held nothing back from you. They've told you everything they know. Now it's your decision."

"Let's vote!" someone shouted from the floor.

Nicole pointed to the next person at the microphone.

"I propose we pass to the vote," he said.

When she asked if people wanted to end the discussion, three-quarters of them raised their hands. "All right, we'll proceed to the vote. Please return after you cast your ballot outside in the corridor."

As the crowd pressed its way to the doors, Nicole turned to Leduc. "It was a mistake not to recommend rejection. I'd rather be criticized for doing something I believe is right, than for not fulfilling my responsibilities. I let people down."

He thrust the palm of his hand towards her. "I was only trying to make things easier for you and your committee."

The colour in her cheeks rose. "You don't lead by standing off to the side when you know what has to be done." She pushed her chair back and headed out to vote.

It took fifty minutes to complete the count. Most people were in their seats when Nicole called for order. "Here are the results. In favour 190. Opposed 513. The offer is rejected by a margin of 73 per cent."

A cheer filled the room. Some people high fived each other, while others sat quietly and exchanged worried looks.

"If we want something better, we need to send a powerful message," she said. "Even if you voted for the offer, I'm asking you to give us a strong strike mandate. We're in a battle here and need to show unity."

People began moving to the doors once again. Alex leaned over and said, "We should've recommended voting no. If we had, the rejection would've been even stronger."

Nicole nodded in agreement, but the lump in her throat prevented her from speaking.

The room was only half full when she announced that 71 per cent backed strike action if necessary. She phoned Goyette and relayed the results of the vote.

"I'm sorry to hear that," he said, then ended the call.

Low-lying banks of grey cloud had settled in by the time Nicole left the hotel and walked towards her car. She noticed her gym bag on the rear seat and checked her watch. There was still time to squeeze in a swim.

She headed east along Côte-de-Liesse. The feeling of shame and anger at not having made a recommendation on the offer continued to gnaw at her. She pounded the passenger's seat with her fist, then turned on the radio to distract herself. A news reporter was describing a confrontation between demonstrators and police at a downtown hotel where a two-day meeting of foreign ministers from the G8 had occurred earlier in the day. By the time she arrived at the sports centre, there was a sprinkle of rain.

The pool was divided into lanes, and Nicole noticed one with a single swimmer who appeared reasonably fast. She pulled down her goggles and slipped into the water. It was cool but refreshing. Fifteen minutes later, the stiffness in her shoulders had dissolved, and her legs felt strong. She focused on her stroke, and the tension drained from her body. On the ninety-sixth lap, she increased the tempo and pushed hard for the last few lengths. When she climbed out of the pool, her stress was gone, replaced by a feeling of relaxed exhaustion.

She showered and dressed, then walked toward the exit along a hallway dotted with the offices of different sports teams. Every door was closed except one. She noticed a desk and a mesh bag with water polo balls in a corner of the room. Two young men sat on chairs talking. One of them had reddish-brown hair and noticeable biceps peeking out from the sleeves of his blue T-shirt. The image was fleeting, but magnetic, drawing her back in time to someone he resembled. She had worked hard to bury this part of her past, but it resurfaced several months ago when Elsie Bernier mentioned Gabriel Nadeau.

Nicole mounted the stairs at the end of the hallway. Once outside, she glanced at her phone. There was one voicemail. After tossing her gym bag in the rear of the car, she slid into the front seat and buckled up, then listened to the message.

"Hi, Mom. I've been arrested. Not only me, lots of people. We were at a rally. Anyway, I'm fine, don't worry. Some lawyers are working to get us released. There's nothing you can do, but I just wanted you to know why I'm not home. I didn't do anything wrong, Mom. See you soon."

Nicole couldn't believe what she'd heard and replayed the message. After it ended, she sat motionless in the car, staring through the windshield. How could Julie have let herself get mixed up in something like this?

The laughter of three teenage girls walking by on the sidewalk seeped in, and a sense of urgency replaced shock. Nicole started the car, checked the side-view mirror, and lurched away from the curb.

After parking opposite the apartment, she snatched her bag from the rear seat and raced up the outer staircase. She fumbled with her keys, unlocked the door, and called Julie's name. There was no response. She ran some water in the bathroom, splashed her face, and grabbed a towel.

As she was heading to the kitchen, the front door opened, and Julie walked in carrying her backpack. Nicole rushed down the hallway and hugged her daughter.

"Are you okay, honey?"

"I'm fine, Mom."

Nicole stepped back and looked her over. "How did this happen?"

Julie stared at her mother for a moment. "I found some people who think like me."

"Thinking is one thing, but getting arrested?"

Julie set down her backpack. "Everything happened so fast. There was a meeting of the G8 foreign ministers at a downtown hotel, and a coalition of groups organized a protest rally demanding they cut the debt of Third World countries. When we got close to the front doors of the hotel, there was some pushing and shoving. I was in the middle of the crowd, and the next thing I knew, someone grabbed me from behind. Two cops marched me to a police van parked around the corner and pushed me inside. I didn't do anything."

"You should have told me you were going to something like this."

Julie unzipped her knapsack and pulled out a creased piece of paper. "Look at this, Mom. It's the leaflet we handed out."

She passed it to Nicole, stuck her finger next to several bullet points, and began reading the first one.

"According to the United Nations, over sixty million children do not attend primary school, often because there is no school nearby or because they are forced to work and help support their families. Almost eight hundred and seventy million people in the world suffer from chronic malnutrition, twenty-five times the population of Canada. Every day, seventeen thousand children on this planet under the age of five die from preventable diseases, like pneumonia, diarrhea, and malaria."

She stopped reading. "Can you imagine? It doesn't have to be this way. The people at the rally were asking the foreign ministers of the wealthiest countries to stop demanding the poorest nations repay debts that have become unpayable because of exorbitant interest rates. This money could be used to tackle these problems, but instead, it's syphoned off into the bank accounts of the wealthiest people in the world. If this doesn't change, it's only going to get worse. That's why I was there today."

"Honey, you should be careful. Even if it's for a just cause, you don't want to end up with a criminal record."

"Don't worry, Mom. The lawyers say the police overreacted, and once everything gets sorted out, there's a good chance the charges against us will be dropped."

Nicole took a deep breath and hugged her again. "Are you hungry?"

"Famished."

"You go and clean up. I'll get something started."

Julie walked down the hallway, then stopped and turned around.

"Mom?"

"Uh-huh."

"Are you still proud of me?"

Nicole nodded and forced a smile. As the bathroom door closed, tears welled up. She wiped them away, took a tourtière from the fridge and turned on the oven.

# Chapter 30

Martin Goyette swivelled in his chair and stared out the office window. A smile spread across his lips. One of his favourite moments at the hotel last evening was watching his wife regale two other couples at their table with the tale of how they mistakenly headed down a slope at Val d'Isère in the midst of a local ski competition during their last vacation in the French Alps.

The meal at the Ritz Carlton had been part of a gala ball in support of the annual Helping Hand campaign. The umbrella organization was responsible for dispensing charitable donations to over three hundred community agencies and projects in the greater Montreal area. The event wrapped up another successful year of fundraising and was attended by luminaries from the corporate, cultural, sporting, and political establishment.

Claire had looked stunning in a form-fitting olive gown. This year she served as vice-chair of the media relations committee, and Goyette made a special effort to increase the participation of the company's workforce in the campaign. He assigned Isabelle Gagnon, Tanner and Ward's head of Marketing, to organize a team of volunteers who approached everyone for donations. While this was the backbone of the effort, special fundraising activities were also organized, including a car wash, a volleyball tournament, and a cabaret featuring the musical talents of employees.

All levels of management were encouraged to show leadership in the campaign. Goyette tried to set the example himself by helping wash cars, refereeing the tournament, and speaking briefly at the cabaret. In addition to employee contributions and revenue from the special events, the company donated $25,000, bringing the total to $150,000, a forty per cent increase from the previous year.

During the awards portion of the gala, Goyette had proudly accepted a plaque honouring Tanner and Ward as the company having made the largest increase in its contribution to the annual campaign. In his brief acceptance speech, he made a point of thanking the company's employees for their generosity, teamwork, and spirit of community involvement.

He leaned back in his chair and reread the press coverage Isabelle had shown him first thing this morning. At his suggestion, she was busy posting photocopies throughout the plant.

Annie had asked Nicole if she was free for lunch in the cafeteria and told her to put on blinders when she set off, to avoid being distracted like last time.

After spotting her friend at a table, Nicole grabbed a salad and joined her.

"Busy?" Annie asked.

"There's a meeting this afternoon to discuss what we do next. I'm still angry at myself for letting Leduc talk us out of recommending rejection. That was a mistake."

"Yeah, some people weren't happy about it, myself included," Annie said. "But we know the negotiating committee wasn't in favour of the offer, so people still have confidence in you. Just don't let it happen again, or this may be your last luncheon invitation."

"No problem. I learned my lesson. That was quite a day. After the meeting, I got a call from Julie, telling me she'd been arrested."

Annie's mouth popped open. "Why? What happened?"

Nicole recounted the events and asked that she keep them to herself as Alex approached their table. He set down his tray, and Nicole glanced up at him. "You're late for lunch," she said, then looked over at Annie. "See, I'm not the only one who has trouble making it here on time." She turned back to Alex. "What's your excuse?"

"Someone showed me the articles on the Helping Hand affair at the Ritz Carlton posted up around the plant. I was reading about what a caring corporate citizen Tanner and Ward is. Now, why don't we see that in these negotiations?"

"Good point."

Alex sat down and squirted vinegar on his fries. "The company milks its employees for all they're worth, throws in a few bucks of its own, then walks away with valuable tax credits and favourable publicity to bolster its image. Not a bad trick." He sampled the meatloaf on his plate. "All the major companies back charities as a cost-saving measure. It's cheaper than being taxed to help provide these services as rights. Meanwhile, they can masquerade as do-gooders."

"What pisses me off is the idea that charity is a good thing," Annie said. "It isn't. It's humiliating."

Nicole and Alex stopped eating and stared at her.

"My dad worked in construction. One day some scaffolding collapsed. He was lucky and survived. But after a long stay in hospital, he never worked again. He got a disability pension, but with four kids under the age of eighteen, it was rough for him and my mother. We used to receive second-hand clothes, Christmas baskets, things like that. It made us feel like losers. No one should have to rely on charity to get by."

# Chapter 31

The last members of the support committee had just left the union office and returned to their departments when the phone rang.

"Nicole?"

"Yes."

"This is Martin Goyette. I've been informed you're telling your members to leave work at two o'clock today. Is that correct?"

Her body stiffened. Members of the support committee had been summoned to the union office only twenty minutes ago, then sent back to inform those in their departments. Word travelled fast.

"The company has suspended negotiations. Our members want to see the talks resume and—"

"You haven't answered my question," Goyette said. "Are you calling your members out at two o'clock today?"

"It's in everyone's interest to restart these talks as soon as possible."

"Let me be perfectly clear, Nicole. If you have instructed people to walk out, we consider that strike action and will react accordingly."

"This is not a strike. The second shift will report to work as usual."

"I'm warning you one last time. Do not proceed with this action. We will respond to any such escalation on your part, and you will be responsible for the consequences."

The line went dead.

Simon leaned through the doorway. "Are you ready?"

"Yeah." Nicole followed him into the main room on shaky legs. Alex and the union's vice-president, Vincent Legault, were seated at a table.

"That call was from Martin Goyette. He knows about the walkout and considers it a strike."

Vincent smacked the tabletop with the palm of his hand. "How the hell did he find out so fast?"

Nicole dropped onto a chair. "Goyette asked me to call it off. I assured him the second shift is coming in, but he may try and lock folks out." She pushed a strand of hair behind her ear. "As people are heading for the turnstiles, explain we're in a legal position to use pressure tactics. Make sure everyone understands this is not a strike, and they should report for their regular shift tomorrow morning." She looked at Alex and Vincent. "Simon and I will take the rear entrance if you two cover the front. Once everybody is out, let's meet back here."

Standing inside the ten-foot-high wire fence separating the plant from the rear parking lot, Nicole and Simon called people over as they left the building. Small clusters soon grew into dozens of bodies pressing forward as the situation was explained to them. After a minute or two, they broke away and headed to their cars as the next group came out and was spoken to.

When the last stragglers had cleared the turnstiles, Simon and Nicole re-entered the plant and walked down the central aisle. The place was eerily silent. On the left, two Propulsion engines stood upright on their pods, one partially dismantled, the other ready to strip. They walked past rows of workbenches with flickering computer screens and empty chairs.

The flash of a white shirt caught Nicole's attention, and she recognized Dominic Rosario as he strode out of the foreman's office and along the hallway. He turned right at the wash, pushed his way through the heavy plastic doors, and disappeared.

Alex and Vincent were waiting at the union office.

"How did it go?" Alex asked her.

"Okay. A few people had questions, but most were just happy to head home early. And you?"

"The same."

"The real test comes now," Nicole said. "Is the company going to allow the second shift in or lock them out?"

She returned to the rear of the plant along with Simon, where they peered through the fence. Only the cars of the office workers and management personnel were scattered across the vast parking lot.

Soon, vehicles began to arrive, and those on second shift started their trek towards the rear entrance. As Nicole and Simon watched, the first people to approach the turnstiles placed the bar code of their employee cards against the readers. The half-dozen metal bars rotated to the right, and bodies emerged on their side of the fence.

# Chapter 32

When Nicole arrived at the plant the following morning, two navy blue vans with the name Samson Security on the side were stationed in the front parking lot. A metal fence had been erected overnight, separating company property from the sidewalk.

Someone in a blue jacket was stopping each vehicle as it entered the lot. When Nicole reached him, he asked to see her employee card.

"What's happening here?"

"Just keep moving," he said and motioned her on.

The line of cars waiting to enter the parking lot continued to grow as more people arrived for work. Meanwhile, the company's own security guards were nowhere in sight. Nicole figured they must be watching on monitors in their underground bunker.

At the cafeteria, she joined others in the queue for coffee. One topic dominated the discussion. Why had the company hired an outside security firm and installed a fence? Was management preparing for a lockout?

Subdued exchanges replaced the usual buzz of relaxed conversation. People had discovered they were on a precipice and feared looking over the edge.

Despite Goyette's threat to consider Wednesday's early exit a strike, the company did not impose a lockout. By Friday morning, the mood inside the plant had lightened, but not everyone shared that sentiment. A delegation of workers from the wash arrived at the union office during break time. Nicole invited them into the meeting room, where Pierre Miron acted as spokesman.

"Don't get us wrong, Nicole. We're not in favour of what the company's trying to do in these negotiations," he said. "But we don't have papers like the assemblers, inspectors, and tradespeople. We can't easily find other jobs that'll pay us what we make here. I mean, myself, I've got two young kids and a wife at home, and we're just getting by with my wage and the overtime I do. If the company locks us out or starts laying off, many of us will be up shit creek, if you'll pardon the language. We want this settled on the best possible terms, but we can't afford a strike, a lockout, or layoffs."

As he spoke, Nicole glanced at those surrounding him. The faces reflected concern, and the eyes sought reassurance.

"I understand where you're coming from," she said. "Our goal is to get an offer people can accept and conclude this as quickly as possible. But we have a problem." She tried to choose her words carefully. "The company hasn't returned to the bargaining table since we rejected its last offer. We've been mandated to go back and get a better one. If we don't step up the pressure, there will be no better offer. No one's doing overtime, but engines are still going out the door. From what we can see, nothing new is coming in.

"It'll just be a matter of time until the work dries up, and they can either lay us off or lock us out. The time to act is now, while we can still squeeze them. They have deadlines to meet and face financial penalties if they can't deliver engines on time for their customers. That's why we had everyone clock out early on Wednesday, and we'll need to escalate those kinds of actions if we want a better offer."

The eyes of some had narrowed, while the gaze of others had shifted to the floor.

"We don't want an escalation, Nicole. We want a settlement," Miron said.

"We can have a settlement today, Pierre, but we'll have to give in on everything. Is this what you want? At the last meeting, seventy-three per cent of our members told us to stand firm and push back. That's what these actions are designed to do. If you have any other suggestions, I'm willing to listen."

No one spoke.

"I know everyone's under pressure," she said, "but we need to stay united if we want to resolve this on terms our members can live with. Let's stick together and fight for that."

Miron turned to his right, then to his left, and surveyed those around him. "Okay, Nicole. No strike, no lockout, no layoffs, and a better offer. We can agree on that."

"It's what I'm hoping for," she said, "but there are no guarantees, Pierre. The only thing I'm sure of is that without more action on our part, there will be no better offer."

Nicole extended her hand, and he shook it. After they trooped out of the room, she returned to her office, sucked in a lungful of air, and exhaled slowly. Her shoulders relaxed, but the feeling of unease in the pit of her stomach remained. She knew she would replay her exchange with these guys multiple times before calling it a day. She couldn't fail them. But she couldn't win for them either. They were all in this together.

# Chapter 33

Following the early clock-out, an email from Human Resources was sent to the unionized office staff. "In the event of a labour conflict with Local 1210, you are expected to perform your normal duties. We will take whatever steps are necessary to ensure your ability to do so. Any failure to report as scheduled will result in disciplinary measures. Thank you for your cooperation."

Monday morning, Yvan Fournier, president of the office workers union, sent Nicole a copy of the company statement along with a note. "Can you attend our next monthly meeting? That could help ease concerns about who's responsible for what's going on."

"I'd be glad to, Yvan. Just tell me when and where," she wrote back.

Shortly after eleven o'clock, members of the support committee were told to report to the union office.

"We want people to clock out of the plant at eleven-thirty," Nicole said. "We don't know how management will react. After Wednesday's action, the company declared everyone's pay would be docked for the time missed but didn't lock us out. Hopefully, it will be the same today. Explain we're not going on strike but simply using pressure tactics to get the company back to the bargaining table. And regardless of what the supervisors say, make sure everyone understands they should report to work, as usual, tomorrow morning."

"What happens if people aren't allowed in?" someone said.

"Members of the negotiating committee and the executive will be out at the gates today and again tomorrow morning. We'll deal with whatever happens and inform people about how to respond."

Half an hour later, Nicole was standing inside the front gate alongside Alex, as people streamed through the turnstiles and headed to the parking lot. A Samson security guard filmed the scene. Some guys waved at the camera, while others gave it the finger.

Alex and Nicole returned to the union office after the departure of the day shift. They joined Simon and Vincent, who had been at the rear entrance. Daniel Leduc had just arrived following a staff meeting at the regional office when Nicole's phone rang.

"We want to meet with your negotiating committee at the hotel tomorrow morning at nine o'clock," Goyette said, "on condition there are no more walkouts between now and then."

Nicole put him on hold and consulted the others.

"All right, there will be no further actions, and we'll meet you tomorrow morning," she told him.

There was an air of optimism when she returned to the outer room.

"They're feeling it," said Simon. "The walkouts are paying off."

"We should prepare a leaflet explaining the early clock-outs have forced the company to resume talks," Leduc said, "and mention further action may be needed. That'll get back to management and maintain the pressure."

# Chapter 34

Next morning in the hotel meeting room, facial expressions were uniformly serious. No smiles were visible on either side. Verbal disagreements at the negotiating table were one thing. Action on the ground to affect the outcome of the talks was another. Circling each other had ended, and the first blows had been exchanged.

Martin Goyette opened the discussion. "We're at a turning point in the talks," he said. "But there's still a chance to find a solution that would be to everyone's benefit. We need to get back to beating the competition instead of each other."

He proposed they jointly seek the appointment of a government conciliator to help work through the issues separating them. To facilitate this, he requested the union end the overtime boycott and the walkouts. Leduc asked for a pause to consider the proposal, and the company representatives returned to their caucus room.

Alex kicked off the discussion and explained that while he wasn't opposed to a conciliator, he was against ending the overtime boycott and stopping job actions. "Every engine that goes out the door weakens our bargaining power," he said. "We can't agree to anything that makes it easier for them to empty the shop. We're just cutting our own throat."

Leduc replied that such a stance would block agreement on a step which might unlock the current stalemate. They agreed to end the walkouts while maintaining the overtime boycott.

When the meeting resumed, Leduc explained their view. The management team then requested a break. On their return, Goyette said that although the company was not happy with the maintenance of the boycott, it would accept this condition, while exercising its right to impose mandatory overtime on each employee for up to eight hours a month as provided for in the collective agreement which remained in force.

A few days later, both negotiating committees attended meetings at a downtown office building where the government-appointed conciliator, a thin man with thick glasses, greeted them in separate rooms. He asked each party to explain their views on the issues in dispute. After two days of shuffling back and forth between them, he announced that he would prepare a report based on his findings.

The following Friday, both committees were summoned to a joint meeting where the conciliator presented his recommendations. With a grave look and a gravelly voice, he said their differences were such as to preclude an agreement unless there was a greater willingness to compromise. He encouraged them to resume discussions with this in mind.

The third week of November came to an end with the talks stalled. A meeting between the two negotiating committees was scheduled for Monday morning.

# Chapter 35

"You want more coffee?" Julie asked.

Nicole was leafing through Saturday's newspaper at the kitchen table and glanced at the wall clock. "Yeah, thanks honey. I'm not scheduled to be at the new union hall till ten. A couple of electricians have volunteered to work on the wiring and lighting."

"Do you think this will end up in a strike?"

"We'll see if management's decided to pull back when we meet on Monday. In the meantime, we need a headquarters off company property, just in case."

The electricians were waiting when Nicole arrived at the storefront location on Locke Street. It was a ten-minute walk from the plant and located in a u-shaped mall housing a variety of small businesses, from cosmetics to carpeting. She unlocked the door, and a musty smell swept over them. "Let's keep the door open and air this place out."

They did a quick tour of the main room and the two smaller offices. After noting the existing outlets, they turned their attention to the lighting. While the electricians headed off to purchase some material, Nicole waited for the delivery of furniture and office equipment which had been rented earlier in the week.

# Chapter 36

As Nicole pulled into the hotel parking lot Monday morning, the radio announcer was forecasting unseasonably chilly temperatures for the week ahead.

She made her way to the meeting room and joined the others. Her stomach was doing somersaults by the time Martin Goyette led his colleagues to their chairs.

He opened a file folder, removed some papers, and glanced across at them. "In the course of these negotiations, we have offered to double the company's pension contribution for the next two years if the plan is changed and promised a substantial signing bonus if the contract is approved. But there has been no corresponding movement on the union's part. You accuse us of not wanting to negotiate, but the record shows the opposite.

"Your refusal to budge on the issues under discussion has been accompanied by a series of actions to slow down and paralyze production. If that is the sum total of your agenda, we see no reason to continue meeting."

Nicole reached for a bottle of water to irrigate her throat.

When Leduc spoke, his voice was low and reined in. "The changes you mention refer to concessions management has been demanding from the employees. Adjusting some of them doesn't alter that fact. If you plunge a knife in four inches, then pull it out an inch, it remains a stab wound, Martin. And in most cases, the knife hasn't moved at all. Demanding employees pay one hundred per cent more for benefits, scrapping the current pension plan and replacing it with something that may not be there at retirement, proposing a cross-training program that is arbitrary and unfair, filling up to fifteen per cent of permanent positions with non-union contract workers. There has been no change in those demands.

"What have you offered in response to our proposals? No improvement in benefits, a refusal to reduce the time required to reach the top pay scale, and a wage increase which may amount to a pay cut depending on the rate of inflation."

Leduc stopped speaking and stared across at the company representatives. "Our objective from the beginning has been to reach an agreement that addresses the employees' needs. We have been forced to act in the shop because of management's failure to do so at the table. It's in neither side's interests to have a breakdown in these talks. But we need some give on your part."

Goyette leaned forward. "Do I take that to mean the union is not prepared to move on any of the outstanding issues?"

"Negotiations involve two-way traffic," Leduc said. "You're on a one-way street."

The pause which followed seemed to unfold in slow motion as both sides eyeballed each other. Then Goyette rose from his chair. "We're finished here," he said and led the company negotiators out of the room.

The door thumped shut, and Leduc's fist bounced off the table. "God damn it! Give me two minutes to make a call." He jumped up, pushed the door open, and strode into the hallway with a cell phone pressed to his ear.

On his return, he walked over to the opposite table and sat down facing the three of them, then sighed and tugged at his beard. "I've just spoken with Claude Drouin, the regional director. You have already received authorization from your membership to declare a strike, and you're in a legal position to act on that whenever you decide. The national union will start issuing payments of $150 per member as of the third week of a strike to all those who do their picket duty. The local has to cover the first two weeks."

Leduc suggested they take a washroom break.

Nicole's hands were clammy, and she felt lightheaded. They had hit a wall, and the next move was up to them. When she returned to the meeting room, there was a message on her voicemail to call the vice-president, Vincent Legault. She dialled his number.

"Are you still meeting with the company?" he asked.

"No, they walked out of the talks. We got nowhere."

"Well, they've locked us out, Nicole."

"What? They've locked you out?"

"Yeah. At ten o'clock, the company called meetings in every department. The supervisors told us to gather our personal effects and leave the building. They had Samson Security guards everywhere, even in the locker rooms, as the guys changed and collected their belongings."

"I'm putting you on hold, Vincent, till I tell the others. Give me a minute."

When Nicole got back to him, she asked where he was.

"I told people to stay in the parking lot till we reached you. Some left, but most are still here."

"That's good, Vincent. Tell everyone to head over to the union headquarters on Locke Street. We'll meet you there in half an hour."

By the time they arrived, the hall was packed with people. Nicole asked Alex to organize picket squads at the plant gates until those on afternoon shift arrived.

He called everyone together. "Stay off company property, and avoid any physical confrontation with the security guards," he said. "We want to block access to the plant while allowing people to leave the premises. To avoid trouble, make sure no one is carrying alcohol, an illegal substance, or anything that could be considered a weapon on the line."

"I can't take my fists off," someone shouted.

Alex grinned and waited for the laughter to die down. "Then keep them in your pockets."

Following a brief discussion, picket captains were chosen, and the group divided into teams covering each gate. Once people had left the hall to set up the lines, a joint meeting of the executive and negotiating committees began.

"We've booked the ballroom at the Crowne Plaza on Côte-de-Liesse for a membership meeting Saturday morning at nine o'clock," Leduc reported. He proposed drafting a communiqué that could be sent to members and handed out on the picket line explaining the latest developments and announcing the meeting.

"As business agent, Daniel will continue to work out of the regional office," Nicole said. "However, we always need at least one other member of the negotiating committee at the union hall or on the picket line to handle any problems."

They decided Nicole should be available during the day. With no family responsibilities, Alex volunteered for the night shift, and Simon agreed to handle evenings.

Nicole passed around copies of a list prepared over the weekend. "Our priority is to organize picket teams for each shift. We need to call the captains about contacting their squads."

After they divided up the list, and the meeting ended, Nicole checked her messages. She noticed one from Yvan Fournier, president of the office workers' local, and returned his call.

"Thanks for getting back to me," he said. "I've been contacted by several members who say there are picket lines up. They want to avoid any problems when they leave work tonight."

"Don't worry," she told him. "We were locked out earlier today and are now officially on strike. Our people have been told to let everybody leave. We're only blocking those trying to enter."

"Good. Are you still coming to our union meeting today?"

"Ah, damn it. I completely forgot. When is it?"

"At five o'clock."

Nicole was the first scheduled speaker at the monthly meeting of the office workers' local. She gave a brief summary of the negotiations before repeating her remarks in English. When Fournier opened the floor to discussion, a stocky man with a neatly trimmed beard raised his hand.

"Thanks for the update," he said. "Those of us here are sympathetic to your cause. We know that next year when our contract is up, the company's going to try and force similar concessions on us. But legally speaking, we can't refuse to cross your picket line because our collective agreement remains in force. According to the Labour Code, the company can't order us to carry out your members' work, but we're still obliged to do our own jobs. I don't want to cross your picket line, and I know other people are worried about what might happen if they show up. What's your advice?"

Before Nicole could respond, Fournier spoke.

"It's in our interest to support Local 1210 for the reasons you mentioned. Our contract has no clause giving us the right to refuse to cross a picket line. But many of our members still have sick time and vacation days that can be used to stay away from work. I'm encouraging you to use them and avoid cross-ing the line. Our executive committee met earlier today, and we'll be phoning everyone this evening to recommend that course of action. No one knows how long this situation will continue, but at least for the next few days, we're suggesting our members find ways to avoid coming into work. That should help grind everything to a halt and put additional pressure on the company."

Nicole turned to Fournier. "Thank you, Yvan. We appreciate what you and your executive are doing. For our part, we want to avoid any incidents between members of our respective locals.

"Our goal is to make sure no engines leave that facility. The company will face financial penalties if it can't meet the delivery dates of its customers. We hope that will force it back to the table and a negotiated settlement.

"We know that if you go into work, you won't be doing our members' jobs, only your own. The problem is that what you do, whether it's ordering parts, checking schemes, or scheduling work, contributes to getting engines out the door. This is what we're trying to stop. So the best way to help us is by not doing your jobs either. Using sick days or vacation time to avoid work would be appreciated.

"We're asking our members to follow the lead of their picket captains and act in a disciplined fashion on the line. But as you can imagine, there are strong feelings out there. Over the years, frustrations build up. When you're picketing in freezing temperatures because the company put you out on the street, you remember those issues and see this as your chance to get some payback. We're trying to harness that sentiment in a positive way."

Following the meeting, Nicole visited the picket lines, which were now staffed by those on second shift. People were buoyed by news of support from the office workers union.

On the drive home, she swore out loud when someone cut into her lane without signalling. If she ever needed a swim, it was now. But that was not an option at the moment.

She found a note from Julie explaining a class had been rescheduled, and she would not be home for dinner. Nicole reheated some stew. Then she ran a bath and soaked for half an hour, her cell phone nearby in case anyone called. She sank down in the tub, basking in the warm water. Suddenly a disturbing image popped into her head, and a sullen Robert Simard reminded her that he would be around to pick up the pieces when this was all over.

# Chapter 37

By five o'clock in the morning, Nicole was bundled up in a housecoat and seated at the kitchen table, munching toast slathered with peanut butter. A first sip of coffee gave her the courage to check the temperature on her cell phone. The forecast was for a high of minus five centigrade, not counting the wind chill. She hauled out long underwear and thick socks, then chose a flannel shirt and denim jeans to go with her black tuque, blue hooded jacket, lined gloves, and low-heeled winter boots.

She left home forty-five minutes earlier than usual, and there was little traffic on the Met. During the short walk from the union hall to the picket line, northeasterly gusts of cold air nudged her forward, and twisting threads of snowflakes skittered across her path.

They had decided all four of them should be on the line for the first morning of the strike when the chance of problems was greatest. Nicole was paired with Simon at the front entrance. Leduc and Alex were covering the rear. It was six-fifteen and still dark when she reached those circling stiffly on the sidewalk in front of the plant.

"Hey guys, here's our relief," someone said. "Think you can hold the fort by yourself, Nicole?"

She shared a laugh with them, and the fatigue of a restless sleep was soon forgotten. By the time the night shift left the line at seven o'clock, there was a steady stream of new arrivals. Picket signs were distributed as more people joined the moving circle.

Security guards patrolled inside the metal fence erected on the edge of company property. The fencing stopped on either side of the entrance to the parking lot.

Nicole removed a glove and dialled Leduc's number. "Are you at the rear gate?"

"Yep, I'm here with Alex and about a hundred others. What's happening out front?"

"Our people are still arriving. No one's tried to enter yet. We're just circling on the sidewalk. The security guards are out in force, but staying on company property."

"Okay. Let's keep in touch."

She felt a tap on her shoulder and looked up at Ben Langevin.

"Morning, princess."

"Please don't call me that."

"Sorry, Nicole. A bit stressed out are we? Hey, I've got a question for you. What do laughter and orgasm have in common?"

"Ben, this isn't the time."

"They both produce a natural high. So, if I can be of service."

"You're unbelievable."

"I'll take that as a compliment. I don't get enough of those." He grinned. "Just trying to lighten the mood. I think you could use a shoulder massage." He held up his gloved hands. "These two puppies happen to be free."

"Don't even try."

As she stepped away from him, several police cars arrived and turned in toward the parking lot. The picket line stopped moving, and people massed in front of the lead car. An officer got out of the passenger's side and walked up to the picketers.

"Who's in charge?"

Nicole made her way to the front of the group, accompanied by Simon.

"We've been called here to ensure everything remains peaceful, and people can go into work without trouble," the cop said. "You have the right to circulate on the sidewalk but stay off company property. When vehicles turn in, we'll ask you to move aside and let them enter. Failure to respect those orders will lead to charges of obstruction. Is that clear?"

"We're legally on strike," Nicole told him. "We have the right to picket this entrance. You're asking us to give up that right."

"No, we respect your right to picket on the sidewalk but also the right of others to go into work. We're not taking sides here, only enforcing the law."

"But if we allow everyone through, our picketing has no impact," said Simon. "We're exercising a hollow right. It's just business as usual."

The officer pointed to the picket line. "Normally, these people are in there working. They're not out here on the sidewalk. This is far from business as usual. You have the right to make your cause known by picketing, and those who are not part of your group have the right to go to work. We're being even-handed here. We don't want trouble, and I hope you don't either. We can all avoid that if everyone's rights are respected. Anyone who doesn't follow our instructions will be charged."

"Give me a minute to make a call." Nicole pulled the cell phone from her jacket pocket and walked a few steps beyond the police car.

As she dialled Leduc's number, Simon leaned in and whispered, "We can't just let people drive in here. We're trying to shut this place down and force the company back to the table."

She shook her head in agreement. "Daniel, have any police cars shown up?"

There was a pause. "Yeah, it looks like several are pulling in."

Nicole explained her exchange with the officer. "So how should we handle this?"

"We don't want to get into a confrontation with the cops," Leduc said. "Let them into the parking lot. But when anyone else tries to enter, we have the right to picket. Just make sure people keep moving, link arms, and nobody starts throwing punches at the police, okay?"

She relayed the message to Simon, and they walked back to the officer. "You can proceed. Just give me a moment to talk to people."

Someone shouted, "What's their problem? We haven't done anything wrong."

Nicole recognized Ben Langevin's voice. "I know. Let them through. Then I'll fill you in on what we're going to do."

People reluctantly moved to the side, and the first of six police cars crept forward into the parking lot. Once the last of the vehicles had crossed the line, and the cops and security guards were out of earshot, everybody gathered around as she explained the policy proposed by Leduc.

Yvan Fournier arrived and said he didn't expect many office staff would be reporting for work, but if any showed up, he would speak with them. A member of his executive was joining the line at the rear of the plant to do the same.

A line of cops stationed themselves on each side of the entrance to the parking lot as the picketers continued to circle on the sidewalk. Shortly after, a police car slowed down and turned in towards the picket line, followed by several other vehicles.

Nicole pushed her way to the front and addressed the nearest officer. "What's going on here? Are you escorting these cars across our line?"

He ignored her, but another one said, "We need everyone to move back and let these vehicles through. Then you can resume picketing."

"No way," someone yelled. "No one's getting by here."

"Hey, look who's in the second car," someone else shouted. "It's Gilbert Larose, the machine shop foreman. They're bringing supervisors through."

People locked arms and closed ranks. The police officers pulled steel batons from their belts and began shoving people aside. Picketers in the rear pushed the ones in front forward. The first car inched ahead, as people shouted and jostled. The line of cops was squeezed up against the lead car. On a signal, they pressed forward and drove people back. The vehicle accelerated into the parking lot, and the others followed.

As the cars came to a halt in front of the plant, someone yelled, "We have to block them!" A group of strikers ran by the security guards and rushed toward the turnstiles. Nicole noticed Ben Langevin's red tuque bobbing up and down in the middle of the pack. She shouted to Richard Beauchamp, a picket captain who was nearby. "Keep people on the sidewalk and maintain the line."

"Okay," he said and told those around him to start circling once again.

Nicole turned to Simon. "We need to regain control and get everyone back on the picket line."

They took off at a run. By the time they reached the dozen strikers blocking the turnstiles, a few were urging those on the sidewalk to join them. Nicole was trying to convince people to return to the picket line when someone screamed, "Here they come!"

She glanced over her shoulder and saw a circle of blue-jacketed police moving rapidly from the parking lot in their direction. Inside the cordon of cops, she could make out the parkas and winter coats of those escorted across the line. Suddenly the automated metal fence beside the turnstiles began to slide right, opening a passageway for the police. Those in front of the turnstiles rushed towards it. Both Simon and Nicole were swept up in the throng. Bodies bounced off the ring of cops, which continued to advance towards the opening.

A police baton held by two black gloves smashed into Nicole's chest, grazing her chin. She stumbled backwards, tripped over someone's leg, and tumbled to the ground. An instant later, she was staring up at blue patches of sky while the shouts of police and picketers moved further away. She raised herself into a sitting position and looked over her shoulder. The cops had succeeded in guiding those who crossed the line through the open gate, which was sliding shut.

As she struggled to her feet, Nicole spotted two bodies sprawled nearby. She made her way towards them and recognized Simon's coat. A policeman grabbed him by the collar and rolled him to the side. A second cop bent down over the other body. Paul Dufour was lying on his back, and his eyes were closed. A patch of red was expanding on the snowy pavement beside his head.

Nicole helped Simon up. He was holding his right arm. His cheek was puffy, and his left eye swollen. "What happened to you?"

"I was pushed from behind through the ring of cops," he said. "Someone's elbow smashed into my face, and I fell. Then other bodies landed on top of me. Are you okay?"

"Yeah, just a little shaken up."

They watched as more officers gathered around Dufour.

"He hasn't moved," Nicole said. "I don't think he's conscious."

The policeman Nicole had spoken with earlier approached them. He pointed to those huddled in front of the turnstiles. "These people have two minutes to return to the sidewalk, or they will be charged with trespassing. That includes both of you."

She relayed his threat of arrests to the other strikers. With no one left in the parking lot for the police to escort into the plant, everyone agreed to return to the sidewalk. Nicole phoned Leduc and filled him in.

Moments later, the shrieking of a siren cut through the air. An ambulance crossed the picket line and parked nearby. The attendants took a stretcher out of the vehicle and rushed toward the spread-eagled body.

Some people were outraged that a former union president had crossed the picket line. Others were shocked to hear his injury appeared serious. By the time Leduc arrived from the rear of the plant, the mood out front was a mixture of anger and uncertainty.

Following the departure of the ambulance, any cars that turned in were discouraged from proceeding further as people bunched up in front of the vehicle. The police were heavily outnumbered and changed tactics. A pattern developed where an officer walked over to the driver, and after a brief conversation, the vehicle pulled away. Each time that happened, the picketers whistled and cheered.

Alex called Nicole and reported the same scenario was being played out at the rear entrance. As the day wore on, it looked as though they had succeeded in shutting down the plant's operations. At three o'clock, those on days were replaced by others on evenings. With fewer people on second shift, the picket lines shrank in size.

Back at the union hall, the remaining coffee quickly disappeared, and a new pot was started. Members of the executive and negotiating committees gathered around two tables in the main room.

Nicole opened the discussion. "Alex is heading home following this meeting to get some sleep because he has to return for the night shift. We need a few volunteers to replace him and help phone the picket captains about organizing for tomorrow."

When the meeting ended half an hour later, the fatigue of a long day showed on several faces. Despite that, people went about their tasks with quiet determination. Nicole spotted Alex and Simon in a corner of the room and headed in their direction.

Simon was winding up his account of the confrontation earlier in the day. Alex listened to his description of the events and shook his head. "This isn't good. It's just a matter of time till the company gets an injunction to limit picketing," he said. "They'll use Dufour's injury and our being on company property. Then the right to picket becomes a joke."

"You'd better go home and get some rest," Nicole told him. "We need you back here in less than eight hours. Call me if anything occurs during the night. I'll keep my cell phone by the bed."

"Okay," Alex said. "Take care of yourselves."

He pointed at Simon's bruised face. "And get that looked after."

# Chapter 38

It was still dark as Nicole parked her car at the union hall next morning and began the hike to the plant. Facing into a gusty wind, she lowered her head and pushed forward along Locke Street before turning the corner onto Griffith. When she looked up, two rows of black-clad riot police were stretched across the illuminated entrance to the company parking lot. Their features were obscured behind plastic face shields attached to white helmets. Dark vests covered winter jackets, and plastic guards protected their legs from boot to kneecap. Gloved hands held long batons and black shields.

Nicole spotted Alex among the picketers circulating on the sidewalk and rushed over to him. "What the hell's going on here?"

Only his eyes and nose were visible under a baseball cap that peeked out from the hood of his winter coat. "Morning, Nicole." He motioned toward the police in riot gear. "They arrived half an hour ago and replaced the regular cops. Looks like Goyette is determined to open for business today. I checked with the picket captain out back. Another group's stationed there as well. I'll stick around after my shift till we see how this develops."

"Okay. If you're not too tired, we could use your help. Why don't you head over to the hall for a few minutes and warm up."

People on day shift began arriving and replaced those on nights. As the numbers grew, the picket line expanded in both directions along the sidewalk. All talk was about the presence of the riot squad. Nicole approached the row of cops and asked who was in charge. A policeman gestured to someone on his right, and a figure approached her. Angular features appeared behind the face shield.

"I'm the union president," she said. "We don't want trouble here today. Our line will be peaceful, but we intend to exercise our right to picket."

He pushed the visor up over his helmet. "You have the right to picket," he said, his words transformed into wisps of white. "But your members must allow people to enter the parking lot when we ask them to move aside. There will be no repeat of what happened here yesterday."

As he walked away, Nicole noticed a police bus and two vans stationed in the parking lot. Her phone rang. It was Leduc, at the rear of the plant. He suggested they call everyone together, remind them to remain peaceful and to link arms if anyone tried to cross the line. After ending the call, she rejoined those circling on the sidewalk.

"Hey, brawler." Nicole recognized Ben Langevin's voice and glanced in his direction, then saw Simon approaching. His left eye was swollen partly shut. "What's the other guy look like, or is he still standing?" Langevin asked him. "Yesterday was the middleweights. Today it's the heavyweights. No rest for the wicked, my man. You'll have to climb right back in the ring with these Darth Vader impersonators."

Nicole called over to Simon, who crossed the moving circle of strikers and fell in beside her. "How are you feeling today?"

"I'll survive. Just a bit stiff and sore," he said.

"You're earlier than I expected. Are you taking a break before the start of your evening shift?"

"Yeah, I need to visit the medical clinic for an x-ray of my arm later this morning."

"Alex is warming up at the union hall, but he's sticking around for a while. Could you join Daniel at the rear gate?" She pointed toward the row of cops. "Apparently there's another group like this back there."

"Will do."

"Thanks, Simon. Look after yourself."

He turned to leave and was greeted by others as he made his way along the line. Nicole had learned his easy-going manner could be deceptive. Underneath that likeable exterior was a fighter, doggedly determined.

People were still arriving for their shift when several cars turned into the entrance. The picketers kept moving slowly in a circle and linked arms. A member of the riot squad approached the lead vehicle. The man behind the wheel lowered the window, and the officer leaned forward. After a brief discussion, the driver rolled up his window, and the cop told the strikers to move aside. They continued to circle in front of the car.

Suddenly he raised his hand, and the first row of riot police pushed through the picket line from behind. They pressed their shields into bodies and struck out at the linked arms with their billy clubs. Shouts and curses rang out as those picketing tried to resist. Once the police had broken through, they shoved some people to the left and others to the right. The second line of cops blocking the entrance moved out of the way, and the vehicles entered the lot. As the picket line reformed, a handful of strikers were holding their arms, while others yelled at the officers, calling them "hired guns."

A white van pulled up and dropped off a reporter and photographer. A moment later, several more cars turned in toward the entrance. People began chanting "Hold the line! Hold the line!" An officer approached the lead car, spoke to the driver, then ordered the workers to move aside. The picketers who were closest to the police turned to face them and locked arms. The cops moved in again, using their shields and billy clubs to separate strikers who tried to hold on to those beside them. This time the scuffling lasted longer before the police succeeded in opening a way for the cars to enter.

Once the action was over, the reporter sought out Nicole for a comment on what had just happened. She explained she couldn't talk to him at the moment and pulled the cell phone from her pocket. Leduc answered her call on the first ring.

"What's going on back there?"

"The police are breaking through our line and escorting cars in," he said.

"They're doing the same thing here. A reporter and photographer have just shown up."

"Listen, Nicole, tell people to stay calm and continue to picket. This is not the kind of publicity Tanner and Ward wants splashed across the front page. It can work in our favour, as long as any violence is coming from their side. Make sure our people understand that."

As Nicole ended the call, Alex returned after warming up at the strike headquarters. They were relaying the message from Leduc to those on the picket line when another group of cars arrived. An officer spoke with the first driver, then told the strikers to move aside. Those in the rear turned to face the cops, locked arms and huddled together, blocking the entrance.

The officer walked back to his colleagues standing behind the picket line and signalled to them. This time the policemen retreated several paces. Then five stepped forward. The one standing closest to Nicole raised his right hand, and her vision was obscured by a jet of white spray.

Searing pain flooded her eyes. She stumbled backwards, gasping for air, bumped into others, and hit the ground.

Someone knelt down and splashed water on her face from a plastic bottle. She could hear moaning and retching nearby. Another picketer helped her up, and they were both pushed aside by members of the riot squad, as cars advanced across the line.

Minutes later, Nicole was bundled into a van that had been driven over from the union headquarters. She was ferried back to the hall along with others affected by the gas. They took turns rinsing the residue from their eyes and faces in the tiny washroom.

Leduc called her and said Alex had explained what happened. He proposed that when the cops told the strikers to let vehicles in, they move aside. Otherwise, the riot squad would gas them again.

Within an hour, the worst effects had passed. Some were still suffering from burning eyes and intermittent coughs, but no one had been hospitalized. Nicole was sprawled on a chair with a bottle of eye drops poised above her head, looking into a hand-held mirror. Her eyelids were swollen, and her eyes watered.

Simon dropped by the hall before going for x-rays and walked over to where she was sitting. His mouth opened at the sight of her. "You look worse than me," he said.

Nicole turned the mirror towards him, "Not a chance. You win hands down." She tried to smile, but the skin at the corners of her eyes tightened, and she flinched.

Her cell phone rang. Richard Beauchamp said a police officer was looking for Simon on the picket line at the front entrance. Nicole passed him the phone and headed off to apply more eye drops. When she returned, he said the cop wanted to speak with him at the plant but wouldn't explain why. She suggested they walk over together.

When they arrived, two officers in uniform and a man in a long brown coat approached them. The man in civilian clothes introduced himself as Detective Houde. He asked Simon his name and requested a piece of identification. After handing it back, he said, "Mr. Arnaud, you are being charged with assaulting Paul Dufour on November 27, 2012."

He pulled a card from his pocket and explained Simon had the right to remain silent, that anything he said could be used against him in a court of law, and that he had the right to retain legal counsel.

When the officer finished, Simon shook his head. "I never assaulted Paul. I was pushed into him."

"You can make a full statement at the station," Houde said. "Please hold out your wrists behind your back."

As Simon did so, one of the cops standing beside Houde slipped metal handcuffs on him.

"Please accompany the officers to the patrol car."

"Where are you taking him?" Nicole asked Houde.

"To the station on Thimens Boulevard."

She turned to Simon. "I'll have Richard Beauchamp meet you there."

"That won't be necessary," the detective said. "Mr. Arnaud will be able to contact an attorney after his arrival."

Nicole pulled out her cell phone, squinted through blurred vision, and scrolled down a list. She scribbled a name and number on a piece of paper and stuffed it into a pocket of Simon's coat.

"This is the union lawyer's number. Call him from the station." She forced a smile. "Everything'll be okay."

The police car sped away with Simon handcuffed in the back seat. Meanwhile, discussion on the picket line shifted from the earlier gas attack to word of his arrest.

# Chapter 39

Simon shifted his body to find more leg room. The shock of what had just happened was beginning to wear off. He closed his eyes and heard his mother's voice reminding him he had a family to worry about. She had scolded him last night as he sat in the living room of the apartment, applying an icepack to his eye. He had downplayed his injuries to deflect her concern, but mounting pressures were beginning to weigh on him.

His mother had been sleeping on their living-room sofa for the past few months after the roof of her small house was demolished when Hurricane Issac swept across Haiti in late August. Just last week, Joëlle had been laid off from her sewing job in a garment factory and hadn't found anything else in the meantime. There were two boys at home, aged eight and nine, to feed and clothe, and a growing need to find a larger apartment since his mother's arrival. His strike pay didn't come anywhere close to covering their expenses. And now he'd been arrested for assault.

At the police station, he was driven into an underground garage and taken to the booking desk. A cop had frisked him before he was placed in the back seat of the patrol car, but once the cuffs were removed at the station, he was instructed to empty his pockets and hand over his cell phone, watch, and wedding ring. He was told to remove his belt and shoelaces, and a metal detector was passed over his body. Then his winter coat and belongings were placed in a plastic bag and locked away.

He answered a series of questions concerning his personal details, before being escorted down the hall to a phone booth where another cop dialled the number Nicole had put in his pocket. The policeman confirmed the identity of the person on the other end of the line, then handed the receiver to Simon and closed the door. Two officers watched him through a window as he spoke with the union lawyer.

When the call ended, he was taken to a small room with three chairs and a grey laminated table attached to the floor. Simon noticed a camera installed in an upper corner of the room. He was directed to a chair on the far side of the table and sat down facing the camera. Houde settled himself in the chair opposite and introduced a second man as Detective Laurin. He was shorter and heavier than Houde and sat off to the side. His dark hair was streaked with grey and swept back from his forehead. He held a pen and notebook.

Houde leaned back in his chair and said they wanted to question him about Paul Dufour's injury the previous day on the picket line. "This is your chance to tell us what happened."

Simon eyed the two men. "My lawyer has advised me not to make any statement until I speak with him in person."

Laurin wrote something down.

Houde bent forward and rested his forearms on his knees. "It's your right to say nothing," he said, "but in that case, you'll be spending the night here and appear before a judge tomorrow morning."

Simon's stomach tightened. The lawyer had advised him he'd likely be held overnight.

"When can I see my lawyer?"

"He'll meet you at the courthouse."

"Can't I be released?"

"Yes," Houde said, "provided you explain what happened and convince us there's no basis to hold you." He studied Simon for a moment. "You've been charged because of video evidence taken from a company surveillance camera."

When he heard that, Simon knew this was not going to end well. He looked at Houde, then Laurin, who had stopped writing and was watching him.

"I didn't assault Paul Dufour, and I have nothing more to say until I see my lawyer."

Laurin scribbled in his notebook.

Houde rose and opened the door. After speaking to someone in the hallway, he re-entered the room and instructed Simon to accompany two officers who would take him to his cell.

They walked a short distance and turned right. Simon passed a series of thick green bars extending from floor to ceiling. Behind them, an older man in stocking feet was slumped on a wooden bench with his boots on the floor beside him. He was leaning back against a cream-coloured brick wall. His eyes were closed, and the chin of his unshaven face rested on his chest. His arms hung limply by his side.

An officer told Simon to stop at the next cell. The second man opened a barred door, and Simon walked inside. He noticed a wooden bench to his right and a shorter one to the left. A small stainless-steel sink and toilet stood between them, and a camera was mounted in an upper corner of the cell. The door clanked shut.

His wife was not expecting him home till after his picketing shift ended at eleven tonight, but he'd promised to check in during the day and hadn't spoken to her yet. To spare her from worrying, he had asked the lawyer to call Nicole and have her phone Joëlle. He'd suggested she explain he was tied up and couldn't call, make up a story about his shift having being extended because someone failed to show, and say he'd be there overnight. He hoped this would cover him till whatever happened tomorrow.

"Here, take this."

He turned around. An officer passed a red blanket through the bars, then walked away. Simon dropped the blanket on the longer bench, sat down and bent forward at the waist. The muscles in his shoulders and back felt like rubber bands about to snap. He slipped off his boots, folded the blanket and placed it under his head, then stretched out on the hard wooden surface and rested his hands on his chest. As he looked up at the bright light in the ceiling, the man in the next cell began to cough. Simon shut his eyes and rolled onto his side. Pain darted along his arm.

# Chapter 40

Following Simon's arrest, Nicole rejoined the picket line. As the strikers circled across the front entrance, a car turned in. They slowed their pace and closed ranks. One of the officers commanding the riot squad approached the vehicle and spoke to the driver, then ordered the workers to move aside. A few people responded with verbal abuse before they gradually retreated. The car crossed the line and parked nearby. A tall figure in a brown fedora and a beige coat emerged from the vehicle. He spoke with an officer who pointed in Nicole's direction. The man walked over and towered above her.

"Are you Nicole Fortin?"

She stepped away from the picket line. "Yes. What do you want?"

"I'm serving you with a court injunction," he said.

Nicole stared up at him as he withdrew a sheet of paper from a manilla envelope and began reading aloud.

"You are limited to no more than ten people in front of any entrance to this facility for the purpose of informational picketing," he said. "No individual or vehicle can be delayed for more than two minutes. Those picketing must not trespass on company property and cannot obstruct, intimidate, or use violence against anyone wishing to access this facility. No other picketers can be within one hundred metres of the entrances or trespass on company property. Failure to abide by these conditions will result in fines of $1,000 for individuals, $10,000 for union officers, and $100,000 for the Metalworkers union for each violation of the injunction."

He handed her the sheet of paper and the manilla envelope. "I expect you to abide by this court order and inform your members accordingly. A copy has also been delivered to your regional office." The man turned away and strode back to his car.

Nicole phoned Leduc, who came around from the rear entrance, took the injunction, and promised to contact the union lawyer. He proposed they meet with any available members of the executive and negotiating committees at four o'clock in the union hall.

Nicole called together those on the line and explained that only ten people could continue to circulate at the entrance. Amidst grumbling and a few profanities, everyone else moved back as specified.

Alex had headed home following the gas attack to grab a few hours' sleep before returning for the night shift. After giving it some thought, Nicole decided he needed to know about Simon's arrest, as well as the injunction, and have the option of attending the meeting if he felt up to it.

The phone rang several times before he responded, sounding groggy. She apologized for waking him, and in the course of their conversation, remembered the message to contact Simon's wife.

After her call with Alex ended, she dialled the number, and a melodic voice answered.

"Is this Joëlle?"

"Yes, who's speaking?"

"Joëlle, my name is Nicole Fortin. I'm president of the union at Tanner and Ward."

"Oh yes, Simon has spoken of you. Is he all right?"

Nicole gathered herself to continue, and in that instant, Joëlle appeared to sense her hesitation.

"Why are you phoning me rather than him?"

That was it. Nicole couldn't lie to her. "Simon asked me to call because he's not able to. I guess he explained how he was hurt on the picket line yesterday?"

"Yes, he was going for x-rays. Are his injuries more serious than he told me? Is he in the hospital?"

"No, Joëlle, he's all right. He didn't make it to the clinic because the police took him in for questioning. He's not allowed to contact anyone except a lawyer, but he wanted me to phone you. It looks like he'll be held overnight and appear in court tomorrow morning. They're charging him with injuring someone yesterday."

"Ay, yai, yai." There was a pause, followed by a deep sigh. "Oh, my goodness. Oh, my goodness. When can I speak with him?"

"Likely tomorrow. The union's lawyer is acting on his behalf. Don't worry, Joëlle. Everything will turn out okay. We'll have him back with you as soon as possible."

She couldn't see Joëlle's physical reaction to the news and didn't need to. Her voice told Nicole more than she wanted to know. Devastation and desperation sounded as bad as they looked. She tried to be upbeat, despite her own concern about Simon's well-being.

Two hours later, Nicole returned to the union hall for the meeting proposed by Leduc and found Alex hunched over a table reading a copy of the injunction.

"It's like you predicted yesterday. They ran to a judge right away."

He glanced up and nodded. She noticed dark semi-circles under his eyes, and the fluorescent lighting gave his skin a yellowish tinge.

Shortly after, Daniel Leduc entered the hall accompanied by Claude Drouin, the regional director of the union and Leduc's immediate superior. Drouin had popped into one of their sessions when they were preparing their demands at the regional office several months ago. He had said at the time he was available to help out if needed, but given his other responsibilities, would not be part of the negotiations and lauded Leduc as one of the union's most experienced and able staff members. His entry marked a first appearance on the scene.

Drouin greeted everyone with a handshake and a smile. He was the top-ranking figure in the Metalworkers union and a vice-president of the province-wide Quebec Federation of Labour. According to his profile on the union website, he became active in the union while working as a machinist and followed the traditional route from steward to executive committee member, then local president, and finally full-time representative. He had been a union staffer for the past twenty-five years.

Leduc kicked off the meeting by summarizing the injunction and explained that while the union's lawyer had confirmed it could be appealed, the incident on company property involving Paul Dufour meant the chance of reversing it was somewhere between minuscule and non-existent. Any defiance of the judge's order would bring down heavy fines which the union and its officers could not afford to pay.

"The appearance of the riot squad and the issuing of an injunction are proof management's decided to dig in," he said. "Reports indicate the company is using supervisory personnel who are former shop-floor employees to complete work on the engines still inside the plant. This means it's only a matter of time until they're shipped out. At that point, the financial pressure on the membership to crawl back on even worse terms will be the order of the day. We can't stick our heads in the sand and wish otherwise. Under these circumstances, our best option is to get a deal done as quickly as possible."

Nicole scribbled Leduc's comments in her notebook and tried to figure out what other options remained. When he finished speaking, she asked if there was any discussion.

To her left, Alex was rocking back and forth, rubbing his hands on his knees. Vincent Legault sat slumped in his chair, and Mike Lafleur was gazing off into space as if hoping for a revelation. She glanced at her notes and tried to put her own thoughts in order but was interrupted before she got very far.

"Nicole."

"Go ahead, Alex."

"What Daniel has outlined is one side of the picture. But there is another side to consider as well. Tanner and Ward has lost significant production over the last few days, and there's been negative publicity that won't reassure their customers who were scheduled to send work here. You don't think they're under pressure too?

"The response of our members has been good. The level of participation on the picket line is high, and people are pissed off at the cops and the company. I didn't hear any of that in what Daniel said. This isn't the time to ease off and cut a deal that gives them what they want. We're still in a strong position to push back. We just need to show we're not intimidated."

Claude Drouin turned his bulky frame towards Alex. "How do you propose doing that?"

"I don't see anything in the injunction that prevents us from picketing Goyette's home. If we notify the media, it might make the news."

"So the company returns to the judge and requests an expansion of the injunction to ban all secondary picketing. Then what do you do?"

"We organize an action in front of the courthouse to defend the right to strike and denounce the use of injunctions."

"I just said they'll ban secondary picketing. That includes the courthouse."

"It won't be a picket line," Alex said. "It'll be a demonstration. We can invite other unions to participate. This practice of companies running to judges and getting injunctions as soon as a picket line starts to have an impact affects the whole labour movement."

Drouin's face was sullen. "Our office has already received phone calls and emails from members of this local who are worried about their jobs, and we're only three days into this strike. One thing I've learned over the years is the importance of knowing when to retreat in order to survive and fight another day. That's where we're at here. We need to reassure the members we can get a settlement on the best possible terms under the circumstances, and that's what we'll do. Now, as I understand it, you have a meeting scheduled for Saturday morning. I propose Daniel give the same report there, and we'll see what the members think."

Nicole jumped into the discussion. "Claude, you mentioned the regional office has been contacted by some individuals concerned about the strike. This is the first I've heard of it."

"I can't give you specific names," Drouin replied. "But the point is, where there's smoke, there's fire. Not everyone who feels like these people will step forward and raise their concerns. Saturday's meeting will give us an idea of what people are thinking."

Leduc turned to her. "I've been contacted by Robert Simard and Pierre Miron since the incident with Paul Dufour. They're worried about where things are headed. And they speak for more than themselves."

"I'm not surprised," Alex sneered. "When the going gets tough, the grumblers and fakers get going. If the people who founded this local threw in the towel every time they ran into trouble, we wouldn't even have a union here."

He looked like a cat ready to pounce. "If you give a presentation that argues the need to pull back and make a deal, you'll receive a response to that. But if you give a report based on what we've accomplished up to now and what else we can do, you'll get a different response. If Daniel's giving the first kind of report, I want the right to give the second, and then we'll see where the members stand."

Drouin glared at Alex. When he spoke, it sounded like he was addressing a mass gathering without a microphone. "There will be no two reports given at that meeting. There will be one report, and Daniel will give it. The regional office is responsible for the conduct of these negotiations, and what Daniel outlined is our evaluation of the situation. The members will have their say, and coming out of that, we'll have a direction to follow. If you can't agree, you should resign from the negotiating committee. Otherwise, you go to that meeting and listen to the members."

Fearing an explosion on Alex's part, Nicole intervened. "I don't question the right of the regional office to give a report to the meeting, but I think the points Alex has raised deserve to be heard by our members as well. If Robert Simard and Pierre Miron speak for others, so does Alex, and I agree with him."

Drouin's gaze shifted from Nicole to Alex, then back to her. His voice boomed. "The members will not see a divided leadership at Saturday's meeting. That is a recipe for disaster. Once management gets wind of it, they'll drive an even harder bargain. No one on this executive or negotiating committee will speak against the line of Daniel's report. If your point of view exists in the membership, it will be expressed by others in the discussion and nowhere else. Is that understood? If you can't accept the right of the regional office to lead these negotiations, you can resign—both of you."

Following Drouin's ultimatum, people shifted awkwardly in their chairs. Leduc broke the silence by pointing out that while the outcome of Saturday's meeting would provide direction on how to proceed in the future, they needed a course of action between now and then.

Nicole spoke up. "Even though the injunction limits us to only ten strikers at each entrance, we can still have everyone else off to the side with picket signs. That will show the company we aren't giving up or going away. We just need to do a phoning of the picket captains and make sure people turn out tomorrow."

"How does that sound?" Leduc said.

Heads nodded around the table.

As people began making their calls, Nicole spotted Alex in a corner of the meeting room holding a list of names in one hand and his cell phone in the other. She motioned for him to join her in the office. After closing the door, she slipped into a chair. He sat down opposite her and yawned.

"My apologies for waking you earlier, but I'm glad you were able to make it in for the meeting. Give me your list to call. I'll handle it. You should head home and get some sleep. We need you in shape for your shift tonight."

"Okay, and thanks for your support in the discussion," he said.

"I wasn't sure what to say until you spoke," she told him. "You did the heavy lifting. I was just your spotter."

"Well, it looks as though Leduc and Drouin are determined to shut us up at Saturday's meeting."

The muffled sound of voices from outside the office seeped in and broke the silence. Nicole leaned back in her chair and stared at Alex. "When I took this job on, I knew it wouldn't be easy, but it's even more complicated than I could have imagined." She rubbed her itching eyes, and the soreness flared again.

"The regional office says it's time to call a halt and count our losses because some people have had enough. I don't know how much the company can be pushed back, but I'm not ready to give in yet. On Saturday, Daniel will make his report, and we won't be allowed to comment on it in front of the members. But we both know people who share our views, and they can still say what they think."

# Chapter 41

In the wake of the gas attack by the riot squad, the arrest of Simon, and the imposition of an injunction, people showed up for their picket shifts next morning full of questions and eager to hear the latest news. Paul Dufour's condition was one topic of interest. There were reports he had undergone delicate brain surgery and remained in critical condition. Another issue was Simon's arrest and whether he would be released or held in custody. But the major topic of discussion was how the injunction affected their ability to carry on the strike. If they couldn't block access to the plant, had the company won? Did they have to give up? What could they do?

With the injunction now in place, the riot squad withdrew, and a small contingent of cops returned. Alex stayed on following his shift and joined Nicole in discussions with those picketing on the sidewalk away from the entrances to the plant. After a couple of hours, he headed home to get some sleep.

Nicole was in the midst of an exchange with several others on the picket line when Ben Langevin wandered over. He hovered on the edge of the group until there was a momentary pause in the discussion.

"Has anyone here ever tried to hook up rabbit ears to a flat-screen TV?" he said.

The stunned silence was broken by Annie. "No, but I bet if we hooked up your brain to something, there wouldn't be much of a signal."

Ben forced a smile and waited for the laughter to taper off. "I was being serious, Annie."

"So was I, Ben."

Nicole's phone rang. It was Simon.

"You're out?"

"Yeah. The union's lawyer got me released at the court hearing this morning on condition I have no contact with any management personnel and don't return to the picket line."

"Where are you?"

"I'm still at the courthouse downtown, but I need to come back and pick up my car."

"Call me when you get to the hall. We can meet there. I'll fill you in on the latest developments before you head home."

"Okay. See you then."

"Simon?"

"Uh-huh."

"Your wife knows you spent the night in jail. I couldn't lie to her."

"No problem. I've just spoken with Joëlle."

# Chapter 42

Led by the financial secretary, Mike Lafleur, a group of shop stewards agreed to picket the front and rear entrances Saturday morning during the membership meeting. They were to call Nicole if there was any attempt by the company to move engines out of the plant.

Accompanied by Simon, Alex, Daniel Leduc, and Claude Drouin, she scanned the room of familiar faces from the front of the hall. The people packed into the ballroom of the Crowne Plaza were not the same as those who had rejected the first two offers. They had been locked out by the company and were now entering their sixth day on strike. They had seen their primary weapon of response rendered ineffective by a judge's order and experienced a police attack on their picket line. They were angry, frustrated, and looking for guidance. With money from their last pay cheque about to run out, another element of concern was looming.

Nicole began by introducing Claude Drouin to the crowd and said that from now on, he would be working with them to help achieve a settlement with the company. There was polite applause which he acknowledged with a wave and a smile.

Next, she welcomed Simon, pointing out that he had been unjustly accused of assault and was being defended against this charge by the union's lawyer. He received a lengthy ovation. Then she introduced Daniel Leduc and explained that he would give an update, followed by questions and discussion.

There was complete silence as he recapped events since the last meeting with the company and ended with the injunction. After going out of his way to praise the courage and participation of union members on the picket line, Leduc said they had no doubt surprised the company with their willingness to fight for their rights. His declaration brought cheers and applause from the crowd.

Having given the impression that the union was holding firm, he explained their objective had always been to achieve a just settlement. So far, that had proven impossible due to the stubbornness of the company. But now, thanks to the membership's refusal to back down, they were in a strong position to force management to return to the table and reach a deal. Of course, that would involve some give and take from both sides. They wouldn't get everything they hoped for and would likely have to concede on some points.

"Your union exists to serve your interests, whatever form that takes. We're here to listen to you. Tell us what you want, and we'll do our best to achieve it."

After he finished, Nicole opened the floor to discussion.

Marcel Bégin had taken a seat next to one of the microphones and was first up to speak. "I'll tell you what we don't want," he said, in answer to Leduc's last point. "We don't want to crawl back to the company on our hands and knees, not after what they've put us through.

"Whenever we refuse to go along with what they want, we're told work won't come here, people could lose their jobs, or the plant will close. It's the same bloody story every time we renegotiate our contract. They remind me of schoolyard bullies. I never liked bullies as a kid, and I don't like them now." His remarks drew a round of applause. "If we can't have hundreds of people blocking the entrances because a goddamned judge says so, let's find other ways to get at them."

A tall man with a receding hairline stepped up to the microphone. "I've got three kids," he said. "Two of them need braces. If we're forced to pay twice as much for our dental and medical benefits, that'll cost me thousands of dollars over the next few years, and I'm not the only one. We can't give in on this." His comments were met with another ovation.

Robert Simard was up next. "I agree with the brother who just spoke," he said. "Daniel explained that in any settlement, there will be compromises on both sides. If we're going to make them, I don't want it to be on issues that have a major financial impact on our members."

Donny Taylor followed, wearing a black T-shirt that said Proud to be Mohawk on the front. He gestured towards Simard, who had returned to his seat after speaking. "If you don't want to make compromises on monetary items, Robert, then I guess you're prepared to compromise on non-monetary issues, like letting the company jerk us around with its cross-training program."

Simard jumped up from his chair. "Don't try and put words in my mouth!"

"So, what are you willing to compromise on?"

"Order!" Nicole said. "Donny, please address your remarks to the chair."

"Sorry. Even if the injunction makes things harder for us, we know they're hurting too. They've had to divert engines elsewhere. That forces their other sites to take on the extra workload and deliver on time. The company has lost money, and the public reaction to the police attack on our picket line hasn't helped its cause. I agree with Marcel. This isn't the time to give in. We should step up the pressure any way we can." His remarks produced another solid round of applause.

Nicole pointed to Pierre Miron, who was next in line to speak.

"Many of us have families with school-age kids. Even with our regular pay, it's a challenge to cover everything – mortgages, car payments, food, clothing, school trips, and sports programs. These aren't frills. They're basics. Working some overtime helps. But there's been no overtime for the past two months. Now we're on strike and trying to survive on $150 a week.

"The longer this goes on, the harder it is to hold everything together. I've got a family to support and a job I want to keep. I don't know what compromises it'll take to get an agreement, but that's what we have a negotiating committee for, to work those things out with the company. If this isn't settled soon, people will start losing homes or go so far into debt it'll take years to pay off. Do whatever it takes to sort this out, but get it done quick."

A different section of the crowd applauded.

After a further hour of discussion, Claude Drouin asked Nicole to pass him the microphone. "I want to repeat what Daniel said in his opening remarks. We're proud of the way you've stood up to the company. What I've heard today is that you want to give up as little as necessary to get an agreement, but you want that done as soon as possible. That's what your negotiating committee will aim to do. You have my word.

"What will this look like in the end? We can't say right now. First, we've got to get the company back to the bargaining table. In the meantime, the most important thing is unity behind your negotiating committee. That's what management has to see. Remember, we're only as strong as our weakest link, and our weakest link needs to be strong. Keep up the fight!" Drouin punched the air with a clenched fist, and the room erupted in cheers and applause.

As the crowd filed out, he called the members of the negotiating committee together. "Let's meet Monday at the regional
office and discuss where we go from here. Does that work for
everyone?"

Heads nodded in agreement.

"Okay. See you at one o'clock."

Drouin strolled away, accompanied by Leduc.

Before leaving the hotel, Nicole called Mike Lafleur on the
picket line, gave him a summary of the meeting, and explained
his crew would be relieved as soon as their replacements got a
bite to eat.

As she walked to her car, Nicole noticed Alex sweeping
freshly fallen snow off his windshield and made a spur of the
moment decision. "Hey, Alex, do you have any plans for dinner
this evening?"

The brush in his right hand hung in midair, and his eyes
widened. "No…no plans."

"Would you like to come over to my place for a meal with
my daughter and me, say around six?"

He stared back at her. "Ah, okay. Do you want me to bring
something?"

She gave the question a moment's thought. "No, we're fine.
Just bring whatever you'd like to drink."

He lowered the brush to his side. "What's your address?"

She pulled out a notepad, wrote it down, and handed him
the paper. "Any dietary restrictions?"

He stuffed her address in his pocket. "Only one," he said.
"Not to overeat whatever is put in front of me."

She smiled. "All right then, see you later."

Nicole cleaned the snow off her car and drove to the sports
complex. Following her swim, it felt like she was inhabiting a
new body, one more at ease with the world. On the way home,

she stopped off at the supermarket and picked up a few items for dinner.

The idea of spending the next couple of hours preparing a meal and having someone drop over for the evening was a welcome diversion. Even if the guest was Alex, with whom she had spent countless hours in the course of the negotiations, the context would be different. And who was she kidding? She enjoyed his company, yet thanks to their difference in age, any sexual tension was on the back burner, and they could just be friends.

Nicole was busy slicing the broccoli and putting it in the steamer when Julie walked in. "We're having a guest for dinner. I invited Alex McCarthy. He's on the negotiating committee."

Julie's gaze lingered. "I've heard you mention him. You know Valentine's Day is still a few months away."

Nicole gave her a look. "Alex is old enough to be my father. He lost his wife to cancer a couple of years ago. I just felt like socializing this evening before heading back to the trenches tomorrow."

Her daughter flexed an eyebrow. "You don't have to justify yourself to me. In any case, I won't be in your way. I'm off to a party later on."

Shortly after, Alex arrived with a bottle of Beaujolais, and Nicole poured them both a glass. They were chatting at the kitchen table when Julie walked in on them.

"Hi, you must be Alex. I'm Julie." She extended her hand.

He rose from his chair and grinned. "Pleased to meet you, Julie."

She smiled back at him. "What accent is that?"

"Whose accent, yours or mine?"

Nicole laughed, and Julie joined in.

"We all have accents, don't we?" Alex ran a hand through his hair. "That would be the remains of a Belfast accent."

Julie picked up a book lying on the table and studied the photo of several young men. "What's this?" she said, flipping the book over.

"Alex brought me that. It's about a friend he went to school with. You're welcome to read it if you want, honey." Turning to Alex, Nicole added, "Julie's studying political science and history at the University of Quebec."

Julie examined the cover. "Bobby Sands. Don't think I've heard of him."

Alex pointed to the book. "Well, if you're studying history, this might interest you."

"Tell Julie what you explained to me in the restaurant," Nicole said.

By the time they had finished the baked salmon and were tucked into the lemon meringue pie, the conversation between Alex and Julie had shifted from Ireland to Latin America and from the Middle East to Africa. Nicole hardly uttered a word. She was impressed by how knowledgeable her daughter was and hesitated to interrupt by asking if anyone wanted tea or coffee.

"I don't believe history can simply be reduced to the actions of individuals," Julie said. "There's more to it than that. But at the same time, you can't deny the impact one person can have on the course of events. Take Nelson Mandela, for example."

Alex nodded. "There's no denying individuals can help shape history," he said. "But historical conditions also shape individuals. Was Nelson Mandela's leadership decisive in dismantling apartheid without a bloodbath? Very likely. But the times and conditions in which he lived moulded him into the man he became and made him the symbol of a powerful movement."

Julie stared back at Alex. Her elbow was planted on the table, and her chin rested in the palm of her hand. "It's been fun talking with you," she said. "How did you learn so much about history?"

"You're giving me too much credit," he said. "What little I've picked up over the years is completely overshadowed by what I don't know. But whatever I've learned is thanks to others.

"When I moved from Belfast, big changes were occurring in the world, including here in Quebec. Apart from my aunt and her husband, I didn't know anyone in Montreal. Other than work and taking French courses, I had a lot of time on my hands, and my uncle kept feeding me books on Irish history. I was eager to grasp the root cause of problems back home.

"After I met my wife, she helped me with my French and got me reading books about what was happening here. As other places came into the news, I tried to educate myself about them too. It became an interest of mine."

Julie's cell phone rang. She excused herself from the table and walked into the hallway.

"Thank you, Nicole. That was very enjoyable," Alex said.

"What are you referring to exactly?"

He looked surprised.

"Did you mean the meal or the conversation with Julie because you two seemed to really hit it off."

"Both," he said, and his face relaxed into a smile. "I've often met students hired to work in the plant during the summer. And I've always enjoyed chatting with them. They still have most of their life to live and aren't weighed down by the past or willing to accept the world as it is. Your daughter reminds me of that."

Julie bounced back into the room. "Natalie called. She's dropping by in five minutes and giving me a lift to the party." She turned to Alex. "I enjoyed our conversation. You should come for dinner again, and we can continue the discussion. I'll try to read your book in the meantime."

He rose, and she leaned in, brushing her cheeks against his.

"Don't wait up for me, Mom." She hugged Nicole and grabbed her coat.

As the door closed, Nicole remembered it was her daughter's turn to do the laundry. "Just give me a second," she told Alex, "I need to remind her of something."

Julie was slipping on her winter boots in the space between the inner and outer doors when Nicole mentioned her domestic duties.

"He's more interesting to talk to than most of my professors," Julie whispered. She finished tying her laces. "I'll probably sleep over with Natalie tonight. Don't worry about the dishes. I'll do them tomorrow, along with the laundry."

That proved unnecessary. Alex helped clean up after the meal and departed an hour later.

## Chapter 43

Nicole rose early the next morning. She peeked into Julie's room, found it empty, and left for the picket line.

A sprinkling of overnight snow had covered the naked tree branches with what looked like a thin layer of icing sugar. They sparkled in the sunlight. The image was so striking that she pulled out her phone and snapped a picture while walking to her car.

After parking at the union headquarters, she made the short trek to the plant, where Tommy Paquette reported that several foremen had gone into work. "I went to the hall this morning to brew coffee and grab some picket signs," he told her. "There was an envelope for you taped to the entrance. I slipped it under the door to your office."

She thanked him, then spoke with several others on the line, before checking in with those picketing at the rear of the plant. By the time Nicole returned to the hall and poured herself a coffee, she had completely forgotten about the envelope. When she unlocked the door to her office, it was lying on the floor.

She opened it and withdrew a printed page, unsigned. The author appeared to have inside information. Nicole figured it might have come from a member of the office workers' union who didn't want to be identified for fear of reprisals. After mulling over the note, she phoned Alex then Simon and proposed they get together Monday morning, before their meeting with Leduc and Drouin.

# Chapter 44

The secretary greeted Alex, Simon, and Nicole with a smile when they arrived at the regional office. She explained that Daniel Leduc was busy on the phone, and Claude Drouin was in a meeting. Then she ushered them into the conference room with its oval table and chairs of imitation leather. Five minutes later, Leduc poked his head in and promised to bring Drouin with him on the way back.

Once everyone was seated, Leduc proposed they discuss the next steps following Saturday's membership meeting. "But before we get to that," he said, "Martin Goyette called me this morning to say the company has suspended Simon because of the charges filed against him. Since his release includes the condition that he have no contact with any management personnel, Goyette insists Simon not attend any further bargaining sessions as a member of the union negotiating team."

"Catch yourself on!" Alex was half-way out of his chair. "Where's the presumption of innocence? The company's trying to be both prosecutor and judge."

"You're right," Leduc said. "But do we want to jeopardize the resumption of talks affecting eight hundred people? Even if Simon isn't present during bargaining sessions, he'll remain a voting member of the negotiating committee and be part of any caucus meetings. No decisions will be taken without his participation."

Leduc looked over at Simon. "How does that sound?"

Everyone waited for him to speak. He glanced down at the table, then looked up at Leduc and blinked. "It's not fair," he said. "I didn't assault Paul Dufour." He paused, and the corners of his mouth dipped. "But I don't want my case to block a return to talks."

"Okay," Leduc said, "that's how we'll proceed."

Nicole raised an index finger. "Not so fast. Simon is innocent. His suspension has to be dropped as part of any settlement. We don't go back in without him."

"We can raise that with the company," Leduc said, "but not now, only after all other issues have been resolved. Otherwise, there will be no talks. Once we get to the stage where we have a tentative deal, the company will be under pressure to drop the suspension if it wants a settlement, but we're not there yet." He looked around the table, and no one spoke in opposition to his proposal.

"Claude and I have spent some time reviewing the situation," he continued. "The supervisors are finishing up work on the engines still in the shop, and once that's done, we won't be able to stop them from being dispatched because of the injunction. They'll have us cornered."

"We may have more leverage than we think," Nicole said. She pulled out the unsigned letter and read it.

"The Montreal plant of Tanner and Ward has a mandate to develop and test the new industrial Hermes engine. The company wants it on the market as soon as possible. The last hurdle is getting approval that it meets environmental standards. Unionized government inspectors are scheduled to carry out tests on this engine at the plant within the next week. Perhaps they'd be reluctant to do so if they knew that involved crossing a picket line."

She set the paper down. "This anonymous note was left for me at the union hall yesterday. If we can convince the government inspectors to respect our picket line, that could ratchet up pressure on the company. I've tracked down their union and spoken with someone who can meet us tomorrow morning at ten."

Drouin shifted in his chair and turned to Leduc. "Would you be free for that meeting, Daniel?"

Leduc nodded.

Drouin stroked his chin. "It could prove useful in reaching a deal."

Alex jumped in. "What about picketing Goyette's home and contacting other unions for a rally at the courthouse to protest the injunction? We can do this before they finish work on the engines and try to ship them out."

Drouin scowled at Alex. "There's no such thing as 'try.' Thanks to the injunction, they can do it, and we can't stop them. It's just a question of time, and there's precious little of that left."

"Listen," said Simon, "most of our members are still willing to carry on the fight if we give them a chance. We owe them that."

Drouin eyed him for a moment, then glanced at Alex and Nicole. "Let's take a short break," he said.

While the three of them gathered around the coffee maker in the small kitchen area next to the meeting room, Leduc and Drouin walked down the hallway toward their offices, deep in conversation. When they reconvened, Drouin spoke.

"You want to try and increase pressure on the company, while we've explained time is running out for us to get a deal done. Here's what I propose. We'll see what comes of the meeting with the government inspectors' union tomorrow, and Daniel can look into the possibility of organizing something at Goyette's place. But that's it. If we delay too long and have to give up even more to get an agreement, it'll be on our heads."

Drouin fixed them with the stern look of a teacher who had given his charges a final warning. "All right," he added, "If we're done here, I have other business to attend to." When no one spoke, he gathered up his papers and walked out of the room.

## Chapter 45

At ten o'clock, Nicole, Alex, Simon, and Leduc were shown into an office on the top floor of a building at the corner of Rosemont and Saint-Denis. Manon Rousseau introduced herself and asked how she could help. Nicole outlined the situation and read the anonymous letter while Rousseau listened.

"Those government inspectors are members of our union," she said, "and they could refuse to cross your picket line if they thought their safety was threatened. But with an injunction limiting pickets to ten people at a time and an ongoing police presence, it's hard to make that case. If the inspectors refused to carry out their duties, they could be disciplined themselves."

Nicole leaned forward in her chair. "Can you find out what day they're scheduled to do the tests?"

"I could try," Rousseau said. She dialled the phone on her desk and spoke with someone while the four of them waited.

"Thanks, Sylvain." She replaced the receiver and looked up. "Our people are to carry out the inspection at Tanner and Ward on Thursday."

"I imagine they'd head off together from an office and drive to the plant. Is that correct?" Nicole said.

"Yes, that's right. They work out of a building on McGill near the Old Port."

"Can you give us the address?"

Rousseau stared at Nicole. "What do you have in mind?"

"Well, we may not be able to stop them from entering the plant, but we could make it difficult for them to access their own office."

"You're talking about secondary picketing," Leduc cut in, "and we don't want to cause any trouble between our members and those in another union."

"I'm not proposing any trouble," Nicole said. "The inspectors can't be disciplined if a picket line at their workplace prevents them from performing their duties." She turned to Rousseau. "Do you know what time they start work?"

"I'd like to help you, but don't want to put any of our members in jeopardy. I think you can appreciate that. Let me call Sylvain back and put him on speakerphone. That would be the best way to sort this out."

After leaving the office half an hour later, the four of them went for lunch in the restaurant on the ground floor of the building. While Simon, Alex, and Nicole waited at a table, Leduc paced back and forth in the foyer with a cell phone stuck to his ear, consulting Drouin. By the time he returned, their soup and sandwiches had arrived.

"All right," he said, "Claude agrees we can go ahead with what's planned for the next few days. Then we'll have some hard decisions to make."

# Chapter 46

Shortly after the security personnel unlocked the main doors of the seven-storey building at the southern end of McGill Street near the Old Port, dozens of strikers poured into the lobby and headed for the elevators. The two guards on duty exchanged glances.

Nicole was talking to Ben Langevin on the fringe of the group to make sure he understood how they were to conduct themselves when one of the security guards approached them.

"I don't know if you're aware of this, but none of the offices open before eight o'clock."

"That's okay," she told him, "we'll wait."

"What's everyone here for?"

"We need to see some government employees."

"About what?"

"An inspection they're supposed to carry out."

"Oh, I see." He scratched an earlobe. "You're a pretty big delegation to fit into an office."

"No worry," Ben said. "We'll wait in the hallway. We're not all here yet."

The guard's eyes widened.

Ben leaned closer. "Here's something of interest. Did you know that during their lifetime, dogs learn as many words as a two-year-old child?"

The man frowned and shook his head.

The elevator arrived, and Nicole tugged Ben's sleeve. "Let's go."

They squeezed in. Ben gave the guard a wink and a thumbs-up as the door closed.

Ten minutes later, the first employees appeared on the third floor and were greeted by several dozen men and women sitting in the hallway, blocking their entrance to the Environment Canada office. Each new arrival was handed a leaflet which asked them to respect the picket line at Tanner and Ward and not carry out any assigned duties at the site.

While Leduc, Alex, and Nicole were present, Simon had remained at the union hall to avoid complicating his legal situation in case anything happened. He had been given a list of media to contact after he received a call from Leduc, confirming the sit-in was underway.

A security guard soon arrived and asked what was going on. After the situation was explained to him, he requested the demonstrators disperse and let people into their office. He was politely told no one was moving. Twenty minutes later, several policemen appeared. The same scene was repeated. An officer left two of his men on the floor and returned to the lobby with the guard.

Martin Goyette gazed out his office window as a handful of picketers circled the sidewalk in front of the main entrance to Tanner and Ward. What a difference from the week before, when hundreds of strikers were involved in a series of confrontations with the police. Although the dispute was far from resolved, he was convinced the injunction marked a significant step in the right direction.

Before deciding to lock out the shop floor employees, Goyette had received assurances that any remaining tasks on the new industrial Hermes engine could be completed by non-unionized engineers and supervisory personnel even if there were a labour disruption. He was scheduled to meet with the government inspectors who were to perform a series of tests starting today. They should have arrived by now, but he was still waiting for a call to meet them at reception.

When the phone finally rang, his secretary told him a Mr. Bouchard was on the line. The man explained the inspectors had been unable to enter their office and collect the necessary documentation because it was being blocked by dozens of strikers from Tanner and Ward. Goyette's shoulders tightened as he listened to Bouchard. "When do you think you can get here?" he asked.

"I'm not sure," the man said. "The police have told these people they'll call the riot squad and have them arrested unless they leave. But there are still discussions going on. It's unclear when we'll gain access to our office."

"Can we expect you tomorrow?"

"I believe so. This should be settled by then."

"Very good. We'll meet your group at nine. Thanks for your call."

After hanging up, Goyette struck the desk with the side of his fist. He'd expected a lull following the announcement of the injunction. Instead, the strikers were escalating their actions and delaying a project with important implications for the firm internationally.

He phoned Sophie Martel and informed her of the call from Bouchard. "How do we prevent a repetition of this in the future?"

"We can return to the judge and request a ban on all secondary picketing related to this dispute," she said. "Our legal team can start work on that right away. We may not get it for today. But we should have it by tomorrow."

# Chapter 47

Martin Goyette was drinking his first coffee of the day at the kitchen table and checking emails on his cell phone when he heard noise coming from the front of the house. It was six-thirty in the morning and still dark outside. He walked down the hallway and into the dim salon, pulled back the heavy drape and glanced out the window. Under street lamps that highlighted the falling snow, dozens of people with placards were walking in a circle and chanting something he couldn't make out, while others were busy blowing long plastic horns. He quickly closed the curtain, moved to the front door, and gazed through the peephole.

"Fucking idiots!" He strode back to the kitchen and dialled 911. A woman answered. He explained that demonstrators were disrupting the neighbourhood and needed to be dispersed. She asked for the address and assured him a patrol car would be sent straight away. Goyette suggested more than one might be needed.

He stalked out of the kitchen and mounted the stairs to the second floor.

Claire was sitting on the edge of the bed, rubbing her eyes. "What's that noise?" she asked, between yawns.

"They're picketing outside our front door. I've called the police," Goyette said.

"Who's picketing?"

"Come here. I'll show you."

She put on a robe and followed him to one of the front bedrooms where they peeked out the window. Dozens of people on the sidewalk were moving clockwise in single file next to a stone wall bordering the perimeter of their property.

As they watched, a white van pulled up and backed into a space further down the road near a streetlamp. A male driver emerged, along with a woman from the passenger's side. After they walked to the rear of the vehicle, the man opened one of the back doors and leaned in. He reappeared with a camera mounted on his shoulder and handed the woman a microphone.

Goyette slapped his thigh. "God damn it! Now the media's here."

"They have no right to do this in front of our home," Claire said.

"We need that ban on secondary picketing. Where the hell is it?" He left her at the window, bounded down the stairs and retrieved his cell phone from the kitchen table.

The dial tone rang several times before she answered in a drowsy voice. "Sophie, this is Martin Goyette. I'm sorry to call so early, but I wondered if you have a hearing set up with a judge on the matter we spoke about yesterday?"

"Yes. I'll be going to court first thing this morning."

"Well, we have more material to submit. They're out in front of my house picketing as we speak."

Faced with the threat of fines and arrests by the police, the protest in front of Martin Goyette's home ended after an hour. It was the main topic of conversation at the strike headquarters all day long. Just before two o'clock, Nicole received a call from Claude Drouin.

"We've been served with papers barring any picketing of secondary sites by members of Local 1210," he said. "Make sure everyone understands that. Daniel is tied up with another matter at the regional office this afternoon, but he'll drop by with a copy later."

"What about organizing a demonstration at the courthouse to protest the use of injunctions?"

Nicole was met with silence.

When Drouin finally spoke, the exasperation in his voice was obvious. "You've organized two separate actions away from the plant, and there's been press coverage of both events. The remaining engines are about to head out the door any day now, and we can't do anything to stop them. We're at the point where we need to sit down and get the best deal we can. There's no more time to play games."

Before Nicole could respond, the line went dead.

# Chapter 48

Gabriel Nadeau gazed out the living-room window of his fourth-floor condo at the fading afternoon light. Why was he so exhausted? It wasn't as if he had swum a hundred laps or jogged around the track for half an hour. He should be thinking about what to have for dinner but wasn't even hungry. He turned on a floor lamp and sank into the grey recliner.

Tomorrow was his appointment with the oncologist, a Doctor Bergeron. Six weeks ago, during the annual visit with his family physician, he'd mentioned feeling out of sorts. A lack of energy, a few aches and pains. So his doctor tacked on some additional tests to the ones she assigned every year. When he saw her three weeks later, she told him his white blood cell count was low and referred him to a specialist.

He closed his eyes and took a deep breath. There was no need to panic. He was only sixty-two years old and had never been seriously ill. Nonetheless, he found himself looking back rather than forward. His best days were behind him.

His own swimming career had wrapped up at the end of the 1970s, crowned by a couple of national titles in medley events and a provincial championship in the backstroke. The transition from competition to coaching had seemed natural. Swimming was his passion. He wanted to pass on what he had learned to the next generation while it was still fresh in his memory.

Over the years, there had been significant advances in strength and conditioning techniques, psychological preparation, and nutrition. Keeping up with the most recent innovations in the sport had been part of the fun. After stressing the necessary focus and sacrifices to those under his tutelage, he would end with the payoff—that incredible feeling when you put it all together and set a personal best. Two of his swimmers had competed in the Olympics, and four had been Canadian title holders. He was good at what he did, and so immersed in his work that the years flashed by.

He fed off his relationships with successive generations of young swimmers. It hadn't always gone smoothly, and admittedly, there were a few disappointments. Some of his charges had the ability to succeed but lacked the drive. Others had the dedication and commitment but not the talent. And then there were the fortunate ones who had it all. He could count them on the fingers of both hands and tried to recall the names. When he came to Nicole Fortin, there was a lump in his throat. She had been his biggest regret. But he'd learned from that experience and never repeated the same mistake.

# Chapter 49

Just after eight in the evening, Nicole spread out on the living-room sofa, grabbed the remote and began surfing channels. As the noose tightened around the strikers, she had started indulging in small acts of escapism to relieve the pressure, like losing herself for a few minutes in front of the television. The phone rang, and she muted the sound coming from the TV.

"Hello."

She hoped her abruptness wasn't obvious but suspected it was.

"I'm looking for Nicole."

"Speaking."

"Hello, Nicole. This is Gabriel. Gabriel Nadeau."

When he mentioned his name, she sprang up from the couch. "Gabriel. I didn't recognize your voice." She was completely in the moment, yet her words sounded detached and far away.

"Not surprising after all these years," he said. "Elsie Bernier passed along your number some time ago. I wondered if we could meet. I need to speak with you and would prefer to do so in person."

Nicole agreed to his request and, despite her curiosity, did not insist on knowing why since he seemed reluctant to talk on the phone. Before going to bed, she took a capsule of melatonin to help her sleep, but it was too late. Her mind had sunk its teeth into the past and wasn't about to let go.

Shortly after five in the afternoon, Nicole walked into the coffee shop on Laurier Avenue and spotted Gabriel Nadeau seated at a corner table, a bowl of café au lait and half a muffin in front of him. His face appeared thinner, and the reddish-brown hair was now grey, but he was easy to recognize.

After rising to greet her, he leaned in and grazed her cheeks with his own. "The years look good on you," he said.

Once seated, she found it hard to maintain eye contact with him. Her hands were moist, and there was a low-pitched buzzing in her ears. When he asked about her life, she kept her explanation brief and mentioned she had heard he was still coaching.

"Part-time," he said.

She felt the weight of his gaze on her and wondered why he had called after all this time.

"I've run into something of a speed bump, health-wise, Nicole."

She watched as he entwined his fingers and rubbed one palm against the other.

"I have leukemia and need a bone marrow transplant."

Her lips separated, and it took a conscious effort to close her mouth.

"The best matches are usually siblings, but that hasn't proven to be the case for me, and there's no one on the registry of donors who's a match. Although it's a much longer shot, children sometimes are."

He stared at his hands for a moment, as if to collect himself. "You left the swim club when you became pregnant and married your boyfriend." His eyes rose to meet hers. "Please excuse me for asking this, but it's important. Was he the father of your child?"

His question struck like a blow, knocking the air out of her. She lowered her head, and neither of them spoke for a moment.

When she felt able to look at him, her eyes were damp, and her voice wavered. "Raymond and I were having sex before I became pregnant. That's what I know."

"So, you're not certain if he was the father?"

She blinked back at him, then took a tissue from her bag and dabbed at her eyes.

"Nicole, I'm deeply sorry for what happened. I have no right to ask anything of you or your daughter. But if she's a match, it could save my life."

She tried to steady her voice. "What do you want, Gabriel?"

"All she needs to do is provide a swab of cells from the inside of her cheek. A lab test will determine the rest," he said.

"And if it turns out Julie's a match?"

"If she's willing to be a donor, it would involve going to the hospital. The procedure is painless. After sedation, needles are inserted in the back of her pelvic bone to withdraw liquid marrow. She'd be home by evening and could return to her usual routine in a few days' time. The marrow replaces itself within four to six weeks, and there would be no lasting effects."

Nicole squeezed the tissue in her hand. "And the pain of telling Julie about what happened between you and me. Will that have a lasting effect?"

He glanced down and pushed some crumbs to the side of his plate, before looking up. "I'm truly sorry to drag you and your daughter into this, Nicole. The odds are slim, but there's a chance this could work."

"If you and Julie are a match, does that mean you're her father?"

"Only a minority of parents and children are matches. But if we are, there's virtually no doubt I am. Even if we aren't a match," he said, "a test like this can often determine paternity."

The drive home from the café passed in a blur. There was no lift in her legs as Nicole laboured up the outer staircase to the apartment. After dropping her bag on a living room chair, she trudged into the kitchen and found a note from Julie saying she would be home late. That was a break. At least it gave her a chance to think this through.

She surveyed the leftovers in the fridge and decided to reheat some lasagna in the microwave. While she nibbled at the tasteless pasta, her mind snapped back to the dilemma she was facing: Gabriel's request to reveal something she had kept hidden from the person who meant the most to her in life. If only she could withdraw into her shell, hunker down, and wait out the danger. But if she did that, what might happen to him? She hadn't initiated any of this. Yet it was her life that was about to unravel, and her daughter would be caught in the middle.

Her appetite had disappeared. She dumped the remaining lasagna in the garbage and walked into the living room. Crouching on the sofa, she drew her knees up to her chest and stared into the darkness.

## Chapter 50

Street lights shone dimly through a haze of swirling snow as a storm blew in from the west. Nicole was in luck and found a parking spot three doors from home. Once inside the apartment, she removed her boots and put on lined slippers, then hung up her coat and carried the box into the kitchen before sliding it into the fridge. A large pot simmered on the stove, and a sweet, pungent smell hung in the air. She raised the lid to have a closer look.

"Hey, get your nose out of there. It's not ready yet."

Julie dashed down the hallway from her room, picked up a ladle and stirred the chilli.

"What's the occasion?"

"Can't a daughter cook a meal for her mother? Besides," she broke into a smile, "I have good news."

"What is it?"

"Remember when I was arrested? Well, the charges were dropped. You won't have a criminal for a daughter."

"That's wonderful news." Nicole hugged her tightly, and tears came.

"Hey, I thought you were the tough union leader."

"I'm a mother," she said, blinking through the dampness.

As they ate, Julie filled her in on the details, then cleared the dishes while Nicole made coffee. When it was ready, she retrieved the white box from the fridge and placed two desserts on the table.

Julie's hand went to her chest. "Wow, what a treat."

"I passed by the pastry shop today, and these two beckoned me in."

Her daughter sampled the syrupy mixture of strawberry, kiwi, and apricot. "Hmm, this is divine."

The tip of Julie's tongue swept across her lower lip, and Nicole found herself looking for a resemblance.

"Honey, I have a favour to ask. Even though you're not responsible for what happened, you might be able to help."

"What's up?" Julie used an index finger to remove a crumb from the corner of her mouth and took another bite.

"When I was dating your father, there was an incident with my former swim coach, Gabriel Nadeau. It was unplanned, something both of us regretted after it occurred. I never told anyone, including Raymond."

The chewing had stopped. Julie's eyebrows dipped, and two vertical lines appeared above the bridge of her nose.

"When I became pregnant," Nicole's throat tightened, and she had to force the words out, "everyone assumed Raymond was the father, including him."

Julie leaned forward, and her eyes widened. "Are you telling me this...this Gabriel is my father?"

Nicole's chest was pounding, and she could hardly hear her own words. "It's not likely," she murmured, "but it is possible."

"So, you don't know who got you pregnant?"

"This isn't easy for me to admit."

"Not easy for you? What about me?"

Julie was on her feet, one hand resting on the back of her chair while the other swept through her hair. Her eyes bulged, and her voice cracked. "Why didn't you tell me this before?"

Nicole reached out, but Julie pushed her hand away.

"Gabriel contacted me through a mutual acquaintance." Nicole paused to steady herself. "He has leukemia and needs a bone marrow transplant. There are no donor matches available for him. Although the chances are slim, you might be a match."

She pulled a folded sheet of paper from her pocket and slid it across the table. "This is the address of the clinic. They only need a swab from the inside of your cheek."

Julie sank down on her chair and stared at the paper. When she finally spoke, her voice was barely a whisper. "Did he assault you?"

Nicole struggled to bridge the gap between then and now, but the words did not come easily.

Julie's voice rose. "Did he assault you?"

"I didn't initiate what occurred between us, but I responded to him and made no effort to stop it."

"Regardless of how you reacted, he had no right to come on to you that way. He was your coach."

The ticking of the kitchen clock filled the room.

"I can't go into this any further. What happened between us should never have taken place. But you have to understand. We spent years together on the swim team, and he was a big part of my early life. If I don't try to help him, and he dies, I'll always wonder if I could have done more. I can't have that on my conscience as well."

Nicole glanced at the mug of coffee in her hands, then back at Julie. "I'll understand if you don't want to get involved. I hope you can forgive me for this."

Julie didn't reply. Her eyes narrowed, and Nicole wasn't sure if the pained expression on her face reflected pity or loathing.

"I can't believe you hid this from me." Julie jumped up and retreated down the hallway. Her bedroom door slammed shut.

The paper with the address of the clinic lay on the table, next to the half-eaten pastry.

## Chapter 51

Robert Simard walked into the sandwich shop and looked right, then left. In the corner, he spotted a man in a blue shirt sitting at a table, a dark jacket draped over the back of his chair. The man raised his hand, and Simard walked towards him.

"Sit down, Robert," the man said. He took a sip of coffee and eyed Simard. "Want something to drink?"

Simard shook his head. "Are you Léon?"

The man nodded. "You have a cell phone with you?" he said.

"Yeah, why?"

"I need you to turn it off and place it on the table."

Simard took the phone from his pocket, pressed a switch, and set it down. "How did you recognize me?"

"That doesn't matter. But I haven't had the pleasure of meeting you until now." The man stuck out his hand.

His grip was firm, and Simard had the impression this was not the first time Léon had met someone in these circumstances.

"Are you a cop?"

His question produced no visible reaction.

"I'm not a member of the Montreal police, the provincial force, or the RCMP if that's what you mean."

"Then who do you work for?"

"Let's just say my mandate involves public security. When protests or conflicts threaten to disrupt public safety, we take an interest to ensure nothing illegal or untoward happens."

"What's that got to do with me?"

"Well, it's not you we're concerned about, Robert. But the dispute at your workplace appears to be getting out of hand. Someone has been seriously injured by one of the leaders of the strike after crossing the picket line. And an ongoing police presence has been necessary at the plant to make sure the law is respected. Now we're seeing other illegal acts, like the occupation of the government inspectors' office and the disruption of a neighbourhood."

"I'm not responsible for any of those things."

"We're aware of that. But others in your union are. Sometimes people in leadership positions have hidden agendas which aren't in the interest of those they supposedly represent. Take Alex McCarthy, for example. How well do you know him?"

"Not well. We certainly aren't friends."

"He comes from Northern Ireland. In the past, there's been a problem with terrorism in that part of the world. McCarthy has connections back there. After moving here, he was involved in a violent strike at a company called United Aircraft. We think people deserve to know that. It would be a shame if the actions of some hotheads threatened the welfare of your workmates or the well-being of your union. We could work together to make sure that doesn't happen."

"What is it you're asking me to do?"

"Just tell people what they have the right to know. We can pass along the relevant information, and you can help ensure it gets around."

The man reached down and retrieved a black leather briefcase leaning against the leg of his chair. He unzipped it, withdrew several sheets of paper, and slid them across the table to Simard.

"This could be even more useful. These are press reports about a strike some years ago. Turns out your union president has an embarrassing skeleton in her closet."

# Chapter 52

Nicole had just poured herself a coffee when the door to the strike headquarters flew open, and Alex burst in.

"Nicole, I need a word with you."

It was more an order than a request. She motioned towards a chair in her office. "Have a seat." After she closed the door and placed her coffee on the desk, he thrust a sheet of paper into her hand.

"This is circulating on the picket line."

She stared at two sentences, followed by numbered lines running down the rest of the page. "Based on article nine of the union bylaws, we the undersigned, request a special meeting to demand the resignation of Nicole Fortin as president of Local 1210 of the Amalgamated Metalworkers Union for crossing an officially sanctioned picket line. Such action renders her unfit for office."

She looked at Alex. "Is this a joke?"

"You tell me. Denis Leclair is approaching people to sign it. He says there's proof you crossed a picket line of maintenance workers on strike at a sports complex."

"This makes no sense. I have no idea what it's about."

"So nothing like this ever happened?"

Nicole slumped down in her chair and stared at the sheet of paper.

"According to Leclair, it occurred during a swimming competition you were part of."

"Oh, no." She bowed her head and covered both eyes with her free hand. "That's what this refers to."

"Refers to what?"

Nicole looked up at Alex, who was running a hand through his hair. She sighed, and her shoulders drooped.

"Twenty years ago, I was competing for a place on the Olympic swimming team at the Canadian championships in Montreal. When we arrived at the venue, there were some people outside with picket signs. I didn't understand what was going on and just wanted to get inside and prepare for my race. My parents guided me in. The day turned out to be a disaster for me. I've tried to bury the memory of it ever since. That's what this is about."

Nicole lowered her head and rubbed her eyes. "I'm sorry, Alex. We have enough on our plate without me adding to it."

He ran a hand across his chin. "Do you have a copy of the union bylaws?"

Nicole opened the drawer to her right and fumbled through several file folders before finding a copy. Alex leaned on the desk as she flipped through the pages in search of the relevant article.

"Here it is." She began reading out loud. "A special union meeting may be held provided a written petition signed by at least twenty per cent of the members is submitted to the president. The meeting must occur within ten working days following reception of the petition, and no less than fifty per cent of the members signing the petition must be present for the meeting to be called to order. The petition must state the purpose of the meeting, and any discussion or action will be limited to the subject for which the meeting was called."

The next day, Robert Simard appeared at the strike headquarters with the required number of signatures. In the meantime, the petition had become the centre of discussion. Annie, Vincent, Simon, and Alex rallied around Nicole. They convinced her to take this on and not give in. The union hall was too small for such a meeting. So a room was booked at the Holiday Inn for later in the week.

After everyone had registered, it was confirmed that more than half of those who had signed the petition were in attendance, and the vice-president, Vincent Legault, called the meeting to order. He read the petition and asked if someone wanted to speak to the motion.

Robert Simard raised his hand. "Trade union policy is not to cross an official picket line," he said. "Nicole Fortin, while not a union member at the time, did exactly that. Her action was the equivalent of crossing our line today. How can someone with that background remain union president? She hid this from the membership when she ran for the position. But now the truth is out, and she should resign. If she refuses to do so, this meeting should vote to remove her."

Vincent asked if Nicole wished to respond.

"I was eighteen years old and headed in to compete at a swim meet which would determine who made the national team and went to the Olympic Games in Barcelona. There were some people with picket signs out front, but everyone was just walking past them. I knew nothing about unions at the time. I'm not saying that to justify what I did, only to explain how it happened."

When Nicole finished speaking, Simon raised his hand, and Vincent recognized him. He rose from his seat in the front row and turned towards those sitting behind him.

"Unfortunately, racism is still part of our world, and as a father of two Black boys, that worries me. But on more than one occasion since I started working here, someone has told me about a remark they once made or an action they took part in and now regret. They learned from those experiences, which were born out of ignorance, and are better people as a result, even though they will never forget that stain on their character.

"What has this got to do with the issue we're discussing here today?"

Simon paused.

"The woman who just spoke to us is not the teenager who was guided across a picket line by her parents."

He stopped speaking and surveyed the room.

"As a member of the negotiating committee, I can testify to the fact that Nicole has stood up to the company and battled on our behalf every time that was called for. She deserves our gratitude and respect, not our condemnation for a mistake she made as a kid."

After Simon sat down, Vincent asked if there was further discussion. No one stirred. "All right," he said, "those in favour of Nicole Fortin's removal as union president."

After noting the count, he called for those opposed. Three-quarters of the people in the room raised their hands. "The motion is defeated, and this meeting is adjourned."

Nicole leapt to her feet. "Just one minute. I want to appeal to those who voted for my removal. We need you. The union needs you. So please, continue to participate in the strike. Don't let this issue get in the way."

## Chapter 53

Nicole was pouring hot water into a filter containing freshly ground coffee when Julie returned from class. Their paths had hardly crossed since Nicole confessed the incident with Gabriel Nadeau. Julie seemed bent on minimizing contact. Nicole couldn't blame her daughter for that. Instead of protecting her as a mother should, she had complicated Julie's life through no fault of her own.

"Would you like some coffee? The water's still hot."

"Yeah, okay."

As Nicole added more beans to the coffee grinder, Julie set down her backpack and turned towards her mother. "I went to the clinic today and got the results of a cheek swab I did last week."

Nicole's hand froze. A car horn blared in the street, and she heard the words, "not a match for him, so I can't be a donor."

She set down the bag of beans and hugged her daughter. Julie remained stiff and unresponsive in her arms. "Thanks so much for doing the test and trying to help. I'm sorry for all the hurt this has caused."

As Julie took another mug from the cupboard, Nicole cleared her throat. "Did the clinic say anything about your relationship to him?"

"I asked, but the woman said the only information she was able to disclose was whether I could be a donor, and the answer to that was no."

Once Julie's coffee was ready, she took it to her room.

Nicole phoned Gabriel Nadeau. When he answered, his voice betrayed no emotion.

"I guess you know the results of Julie's test," he said.

"Yes, she just told me. I'm sorry, Gabriel."

"Me too. Let's hope a match turns up on the donor's list while there's still time."

In the pause that followed, she worked up the courage to ask her question. "Did the results reveal anything about your relationship to Julie?"

There was no response. She bit her lip in the lingering silence.

"I don't know," he finally said. "They only told me Julie wasn't a match. I was focused on that and didn't ask anything else. If I find out more, I'll pass it along."

She closed her eyes and exhaled.

"Nicole?"

"Yes."

"Please thank Julie for doing the test. I'm sorry for everything."

# Chapter 54

Alex placed the last dish on the drainboard and leaned over the sink to empty the water. A familiar marimba melody erupted behind him. He whisked a tea towel across his hands and retrieved his cell phone from the kitchen table.

"Yes."

"Hello, is this Alex?"

He didn't recognize the female voice.

"It is."

"Hi. This is Julie, Nicole's daughter. We met when you came to dinner."

"Ah, Julie. How are you?"

"I'm good thanks. I finished reading the book you left us and wondered if you have any others to recommend on Irish history?"

"I certainly do. You're welcome to drop by and go through my library if you'd like."

A harsh buzzing shattered the silence of his apartment, and Alex navigated his way past the boots on the inner staircase. He opened the door, and Julie stood before him at the side entrance, tucked into a cream-coloured coat. Her face was framed in a hood trimmed with faux fur. She extended a mitten, and he clasped it with one hand while guiding her inside.

"Come in and take the chill off you," he said.

She removed her winter boots, and he returned with a pair of open heeled slippers.

"Try these on. They were my wife's, but they might fit you."
She slid her foot into one and smiled up at him. "Perfect."

As she stepped into the apartment, he took her coat and hung it on a wall hook. The front room contained a beige and brown striped sofa, two matching chairs, and a coffee table. Along the far wall, three cabinets were packed with books.

"This way," he said, and led her towards a kitchen bathed in weak winter sunlight. "A cup of tea to warm you up?"

"Sure, thank you."

He gestured towards two padded chairs, one on each side of a small, wooden table. "Sit yourself down." He plugged in the kettle, opened a cupboard and lowered two tins to the counter. After lifting the lid off the smaller one, he removed a couple of tea bags.

"It's cozy in here," she said.

"Well, when you're on your own, you don't need much space. I moved in six months ago. My problem is getting rid of all the clutter from the past still in storage. I haven't tackled that yet. But enough about me. What did you think of the book?"

"I loved it. I guess that sounds odd when we're discussing someone starving himself to death. His action was so extreme. I'd never heard of Bobby Sands before I read your book. He seemed like a contradictory person, prepared to die for the prisoners' demands, yet, so drawn to life, especially to poetry and music. Is that what he was like?"

"I'm not so sure those traits are contradictory," Alex said, "but in any case, the Bobby I knew as a young lad was a much different person. He was mad about football, running, and going to dances back then. The political path he ended up on was imposed by events well beyond himself."

Julie nodded. "Regardless of the choices he made, there's no denying his courage."

She lowered her gaze, twisted a spiral ring around her finger then looked up at Alex. "It's fun talking with you. I can't have these kinds of conversations with my Mom."

"Ah, don't sell your mother short," he said. "While we're talking about history, she's busy making a little of her own. Did you know she's the first woman ever elected president of our union?"

"Yeah," Julie said, "and I'm proud of her for that. But she's also made some mistakes in life."

"You mean crossing that picket line? She was a wee girl and didn't understand what she was doing."

"What picket line?"

"The one at the swimming competition."

Julie's eyes widened. "I don't know anything about that," she said.

Before Alex could reply, the kettle began to whistle. He jumped up, unplugged it, and poured water into the teapot. "Anyway, that's over and done with."

"Just another thing she never mentioned," Julie said, her voice trailing off.

"These negotiations have been tough," Alex added. "Many a man could have been brought to his knees by now, but your mother's still standing." He set the teapot on the table.

Julie looked down at her hands and said nothing further.

Alex placed two ceramic mugs and a pitcher of milk between them. "This tea will be on the strong side after it steeps. You might want to cushion it with a spot of milk." He offered the pitcher to Julie, then glanced over his shoulder. "Ah, would you look at that now. I forgot the biscuits." He got up and grabbed the large blue tin from the counter, removed the lid, and placed it between them. "You should find something in here that tickles your fancy."

Julie peeked in and withdrew a flat, chocolate-covered cookie.

"A fine choice," he told her and took one for himself.

While they drank their tea, Alex asked questions about the courses she was taking at school. After setting their empty mugs in the sink, they moved from the kitchen to the front room. He went through his library, chose several titles, and watched as Julie carefully examined each book.

His mind drifted. If only he could transport her back to those teenage years in Belfast. Show her the lay of the land. Let her soak in the atmosphere, catch the language, hear the music, see the clothes, smell the dampness, taste the tension, feel the fear. That would beat any stories he could tell. Or any accounts she could read.

Half an hour later, Julie tucked a copy of Leon Uris's *Trinity* in her backpack. "The book you lent us says Bobby Sands liked this story and recounted it to the other prisoners. I'm curious to read the novel myself."

"You won't regret it," Alex assured her. "You can learn a good bit of Irish history from that book."

After slipping into her coat, she tiptoed down the staircase and pulled on her winter boots. "Thanks for everything, including the tea and biscuits."

"My pleasure, Julie. You're welcome any time."

Alex watched her walk away in the dwindling afternoon light. Then he went back to the front room, picked up the books strewn on the coffee table and placed them on the shelves. The silence enveloped him. He returned to the kitchen, put the tins back in the cupboard and stared out the small window above the sink. Julie's footprints were still visible in the freshly fallen snow.

# Chapter 55

Seated before Simon, Alex, and Nicole at the strike head-quarters were three dozen men and women who had shown themselves to be among the most committed and determined in this battle. But there was no way to ignore the mounting odds against them.

Neither Leduc nor Drouin was present at the support committee meeting because of responsibilities at the regional office. Nicole asked Alex to open the discussion on what lay ahead.

He explained that while nothing had left the plant since the beginning of the strike, information the union had gathered suggested several engines were nearing completion. Once successfully tested, they would be shipped out. The only hope of blocking them was through mass picketing. That would mean defying the injunction, leading to arrests and fines, not to mention an all-out war with the regional office.

Nicole opened the floor for discussion. Richard Beauchamp, one of the electricians and a picket captain, raised his hand.

"We've put up a good fight," he said, "but I'm worried that if we don't get this resolved soon, the support could erode. We're getting close to Christmas. That's a time when people need extra cash. At the last membership meeting, we heard from those who wanted to end things as soon as possible. Their ranks will only grow the longer this drags on."

Nicole noticed Ben Langevin waving his hand at the back of the room. "Go ahead, Ben."

"What Alex said reminded me of ants."

Marcel Bégin leapt to his feet. "What the hell are you going on about now!"

"Hang on, Marcel, hear me out," Ben said. "Scientists estimate there are ten quadrillion ants on earth. That's almost one and a half million ants for every human being. I thought of ants because Alex mentioned our power is in our numbers, and if they're limited by the injunctions, then we're at a disadvantage. But ants aren't only numerous. They work together, they have a division of labour, and they communicate with each other. They're problem-solvers and survivors. If ants can do it, so can we. That's my point."

Bégin turned to the person beside him. "I can't believe I'm saying this, but he almost made sense."

Annie raised her hand. "I hate the thought of Goyette waltzing into the cafeteria for a coffee with a grin plastered on his face because we buckled, and he got what he was after. It's true we've all lost money, at least in the short term," she said. "But self-respect is harder to recover. I don't want to lose that too. If the only way to stop those engines from leaving the plant is through mass picketing, I think we have to consider doing that, whatever the consequences."

Suddenly Tommy Paquette was on his feet. "Sorry to interrupt," he shouted. "I just got a text message from Serge Tremblay on the picket line. There's been an explosion at the plant."

Eyes widened, jaws dropped, and the room went quiet. Then pandemonium, as everyone grabbed their gear and scrambled for the door. It looked like a bizarre winter road race, with dozens of people buttoning coats, covering heads, and grabbing gloves from pockets, as they rushed from the union hall towards the plant.

Ben Langevin was off like a racing dog, with his head thrust forward and his long legs flying over the ground, while Marcel

Bégin rolled from side to side, like a waddling duck trying to escape a predator. Nicole cautioned Simon to stay put because of his ban from the picket line, then sprinted to catch up with Annie.

By the time she arrived at the front entrance, there were two fire trucks and an ambulance in the parking lot. A plume of smoke escaped from the side of the building. Serge Tremblay was standing next to another picketer when Nicole reached him.

"What...what's happened?" she asked, between gasps of air.

"Looks like there's been an explosion in plasma spray," he said.

"What could have caused that?"

He pointed to a group of people off to the right. "One of the guys on the line, Moretti, works in the department. Maybe he could tell you more."

As she approached Alessandro Moretti, there was a semi-circle of people huddled around him. He was a short man with a black moustache. His thick eyebrows bounced up and down in harmony with his hands as he spoke.

"We ignite a mixture of gases like argon-hydrogen or oxy-acetylene with a spark and spray a powder at high speed along the barrel of a gun to coat the surface of an engine part," he said.

"So what do you think caused the explosion?" someone asked.

"Hard to say for sure. Could be any number of things."

Necks craned as people looked beyond the fence at the rising smoke.

Nicole walked over to a security guard and motioned towards the plant. "You know what happened?" The man stared at her, then shook his head. "Anybody hurt?" The guard shrugged his shoulders. "Looks serious." He turned his back and walked away.

Martin Goyette was reading an email on his computer when his concentration was disturbed by a muffled "boom." He glanced out the window towards the picket line at the front of the plant and saw several security guards rush towards the rear and out of view. People on the picket line were pointing in the same direction.

Goyette hurried out of the office. He headed down the hallway towards the double doors with rectangular windows leading to the plant. Two people ran past on the other side of the doors. He followed them along the aisle by the machine shop, turned the corner, and stopped dead. A hundred metres beyond, smoke or dust, he couldn't tell which, swirled around an object extending into the corridor at a weird angle.

As he advanced, the air became thick with a garlic-like smell that brought on a fit of coughing. Through the opaqueness, bodies appeared to be moving around something in the middle of the hallway. Edging closer, he saw the sliding door of the plasma-spray cabin hanging off its hinges and, on closer inspection, spotted daylight streaming through a small hole in the outer wall of the enclosure.

Beyond the mangled door, someone was moaning. Several people were crouched around a body lying on the floor. Goyette caught a glimpse of charred skin and open sores where the tissue had been burned away. There was an acrid smell in the air. He recognized Gilbert Larose, the machine-shop foreman, and asked him what had happened.

His face ashen, Larose shook his head. "I don't know exactly, but he was in the plasma spray cabin when there was an explosion."

"Who is it?"

"Dominic Rosario."

"The foreman on the Propulsion line?"

"Uh-huh. He worked in plasma spray before becoming a supervisor. He's the only one of us who could do this work in-house."

Goyette watched as Pascal Drolet, the head of company security, answered his cell phone, then ordered one of his men to meet the ambulance attendants who had just arrived. He approached Drolet. "Was it an accident or something deliberate, Pascal?"

"You mean some kind of sabotage?"

"Yeah."

"I have no idea. The police and Ministry of Public Safety will need to carry out an investigation."

Cold air seeped through the hole in the exterior wall, and Goyette shivered. Moments later, two ambulance attendants rushed towards them, pushing a stretcher on wheels. They knelt beside the man, assessing the extent of his injuries. Goyette watched them, then turned away. The sickly smell of burned flesh clung to the back of his throat. He retreated down the corridor and headed for the washroom.

# Chapter 56

When Alex, Simon, and Nicole arrived at the regional office, the receptionist's usual smile was missing. Instead, they were met with a perfunctory nod. She ushered them into the conference room, then continued down the hallway toward the offices of Leduc and Drouin who had summoned them there. The two men soon joined them.

Drouin closed the door with a thud and plopped down in a chair. "What the hell happened?" he said. "The media are all over us, asking for a comment about the explosion. Goyette's claiming the company has a strong safety record, and he's raised possible links with the strike at the plant."

Nicole cleared her throat. "According to one of the guys who works in plasma spray, there's always a danger with flammable gases. They must have been working in the area."

Drouin studied her for a moment, then glanced at Leduc, who was tugging on his beard. "Okay. We'll tell the press we support a full investigation and remind them that the highly trained employees who normally do this job have been locked out and forced on strike by a company that refuses to treat its workforce fairly."

The next morning, Nicole grabbed copies of the French and English dailies on her way to the picket line. Both featured coverage of the explosion. They quoted the union declaration calling for an investigation, but one article cited an unnamed source who referred to the possibility of "extremist elements" being linked to the blast. The other paper contained an editorial calling for a thorough inquiry while condemning "anyone who might be tempted to break the law and risk the lives of innocent people, all in the name of 'workers' rights.'" Without any evidence, the union had been placed under suspicion of possible involvement.

Discussion on the line had shifted to the explosion. What could have caused it? And what effect would it have on the strike? There was a growing feeling that events were spinning out of control.

In a late-afternoon press conference, the authorities disclosed the results of their preliminary investigation. It appeared that gas leaking from an overhead pipe in the plasma spray cabin had ignited when a tool was dropped, causing a spark. Sensors should have detected the leak before the accident happened, but it appeared they may have malfunctioned. No criminal intent was suspected. Dominic Rosario was reported to be in hospital, suffering from third-degree burns.

## Chapter 57

Martin Goyette hung up the phone on his desk and paced in front of the picture window, hands clasped behind his back. The heel of his right foot began to throb, a painful reminder of his appointment with the podiatrist later in the week. He sat down and dialled a number. Five minutes later, Charles Allard, the director of Human Resources and vice-chairman of the company negotiating committee, joined him.

"Take a seat, Charles. I've just had a conversation with Sir Edmund about recent events," Goyette said. "He's not pleased with the explosion in plasma spray. An accident like that can damage the company's reputation. Sir Edmund made the point that if it were merely a question of resolving local issues, we could take more time with the negotiations, but anything that delays our launch of the new industrial Hermes engine raises the stakes of what's happening here.

"I've cleared my agenda for the next couple of hours. That should give us enough time to review the situation before we convene a meeting of the negotiating committee."

"Okay. Let me return to my office and get some papers," Allard said. "I'll stop by the cafeteria and pick up a coffee on the way back. Would you like one?"

Goyette shook his head. "No, I'm already wired, Charles. Talking to a disgruntled company chairman can do that to you."

While he waited for Allard to return, Goyette's thoughts circled back to his conversation with Sir Edmund. In the course of their discussion, a lateral transfer to one of the company's facilities in Texas had been mentioned, once the negotiations in Montreal were completed. Goyette could already picture Claire's disappointment when he gave her the news. She was so looking forward to attending the West End plays that his promotion to the head office in London would have made possible.

At one o'clock, the other members of the company's negotiating team joined the two men in the corporate conference room.

"I've spoken with Sir Edmund," Goyette explained. "We discussed the evolution of the negotiations, including how recent events have negatively impacted our objectives, both local and international. The changes we've argued for since the opening of these talks have lost none of their urgency. But there are times when it's necessary to take a step back on one front in order to advance on another. Once that's been accomplished, it's possible to return to the first front and push forward again."

# Chapter 58

Claude Drouin motioned to a chair opposite his desk at the regional union headquarters, and Daniel Leduc eased his bulky frame downward. Shelves filled with leather-bound texts on labour law and three-ring binders containing dozens of arbitration cases lined two walls of the office.

Drouin leaned forward and rested his elbows on the desk. "It's chestnut time," he said. "We need to figure out what it will take to pull them out of the fire. Do you have a list of the company's demands?"

Leduc withdrew some sheets of paper from his file folder and set them down on the desk. "The three of them are going to resist," he said.

"Yeah, I know, but there's a greater good here. Once management completes work on the remaining engines and ships them out, all the anger will be turned on us," Drouin said. "You know where that can lead. Someone decides we're the problem and starts contacting other unions. Then we find ourselves fighting a different battle. That's a headache we don't need. But if this is handled right, we can give up less than the company's demanding and claim a partial victory."

Leduc's cell phone rang. He pulled it from his pocket and glanced at the caller ID. "It's Martin Goyette. I wonder what he wants. Should I put him on speakerphone?"

"Go ahead," Drouin said.

"Hello," Leduc answered.

"Daniel, this is Martin Goyette."

"Yes, Martin, what can I do for you?"

"We'd like to schedule a session with your negotiating committee tomorrow morning at nine. We have a new proposal to present. Would the members of your committee be available, excluding Simon Arnaud of course?"

Leduc looked over at Drouin, who nodded.

"Yes, I think we can get everyone together then."

"Good. We'll see you tomorrow."

"All right."

The call ended, and Leduc set down his phone. "Well, how about that."

"Interesting," Drouin said. "Let's see what they have to say. In the meantime, we need a plan. If they ease off on some issues, all the better, but we can't count on that."

Leduc pulled his chair closer, and both men peered at the papers lying on Drouin's desk.

# Chapter 59

Leduc phoned Nicole to say the company wanted to meet. She tried to pry more information out of him, but all he said was that Goyette had mentioned a new proposal without giving any details. She contacted Alex and made arrangements for Simon to be available following the session with management.

When the meeting opened at the hotel, Goyette kicked things off by welcoming Drouin to the talks. He insisted the issues raised by the company needed to be addressed in the interests of the long-term viability of the Montreal site. Despite efforts to reach a negotiated settlement, they found themselves in a situation where production had been disrupted, and employees were without a pay cheque. Neither side benefitted from this, he said.

"Our proposal is the following. We will extend the existing collective agreement for fifteen months from its termination last September and include a three per cent wage increase to cover that period.

"For the next three months, our two negotiating committees will continue to discuss four issues: the replacement of up to fifteen per cent of permanent employees who retire or leave the company with contract workers furnished by a third party, the implementation of a cross-training program to boost efficiency, an increase in the current employees' contribution to the cost of their health care benefits, and making changes to the existing pension plan. Any matter on which we cannot agree after three months will be referred to an arbitrator whose judgement will be binding on both parties."

Each union negotiator was handed a copy of the proposal.

"We'll need time to evaluate this," Leduc said. "I think we should schedule a meeting for tomorrow morning."

Goyette nodded, and the company's negotiating team filed out of the room.

Nicole called Simon at the union headquarters, then went out to the main desk and had a photocopy of the offer made up for him. When he arrived, Drouin was shuffling back and forth, talking to someone on his cell phone, and Leduc was hunched over his notes. Alex had gone to the washroom. Nicole gave Simon a copy of the proposal to read.

Ten minutes later, Leduc and Drouin moved to the other side of the room, pulled out chairs, and sat down opposite the three of them.

"Well, what do you think?" Leduc asked.

"I don't have a problem with extending the existing contract," Alex said, "since that would represent a retreat on their part. But how much are they retreating if we'd still be forced to discuss all the changes they want, and these could be imposed by an arbitrator?"

"Why are the only items to be discussed the ones they raised? What about our demands?" Simon added.

Leduc looked over at Nicole.

"The clauses the company wants to alter are provisions from the past we're trying to preserve," she said. "Maybe the arbitrator won't grant everything management wants on all questions, but any changes he proposes will help them and hurt us."

"Listen, if we agree to this offer, everyone returns to work with a wage increase, and we haven't conceded anything," Leduc said. "We can come back with our viewpoint on all the issues they raise and, if there's no agreement, the arbitrator will decide. We'll have the same opportunity as management to present our arguments before that happens. I'm going to level with you. This is better than I expected under the circumstances."

"The company knows we're opposed to what it wants," Nicole countered. "If we haven't agreed after seven months of discussion, another three months won't change that. With this deal, we agree to accept an arbitrator's ruling in advance without even knowing what that might be."

"The company's in the same boat," Leduc said. "It doesn't know what the arbitrator will decide."

"Look at the recent arbitration cases involving Air Canada," Alex replied. "Each one of those favoured the company, not the workers."

Claude Drouin rose from his chair and walked around the table, so he was standing with his back to Leduc and facing the three of them.

"If we don't bring these talks to a rapid conclusion, it will only get worse for people. We have an opportunity to end this strike on terms we can accept while continuing to argue our case in front of an arbitrator. But you insist on raising objections that could blow this thing apart. As regional chairman, I'm ultimately responsible for what happens here. If you vote to reject this deal, I'll place Local 1210 under trusteeship for the remainder of these negotiations, and this offer will be recommended to the members. Is that clear?"

No one spoke for a moment.

"What about Simon's suspension and the charges against him?"

Drouin's head swivelled in Nicole's direction. "If no agreement is reached, we'll demand Simon's case be included with those issues that go to arbitration."

"But Simon's innocent," she insisted. "Any settlement has to include his reinstatement."

Drouin turned to Leduc. "Daniel, put the question to them."

"Nicole, do you recommend this offer to the membership?" Leduc asked.

"No."

"Alex?"

"No."

"Simon?"

"No."

Drouin walked back to his briefcase, which was lying on the table next to Leduc. He pulled out the union constitution, flipped through it, and turned to face the three of them. "Under article sixteen, section one, I'm informing you that this local is being placed under the trusteeship of the regional office for the duration of these negotiations which will be conducted jointly by the business agent and myself as regional director. You will hereby have no further part in these talks and will each receive written notification to this effect."

# Chapter 60

The day after their removal, Nicole attended a hastily called session of the union executive. Claude Drouin and Daniel Leduc explained the company's latest offer and announced that because of its rejection by the three elected members of the negotiating committee, the local had been placed under trusteeship for the remainder of the talks. They reported that at a meeting earlier in the day, company representatives had agreed to include Simon's suspension among the issues to be discussed. Copies of the offer would be made available within the next twenty-four hours, and a vote would take place in two days' time.

When Leduc asked if there was any discussion, no one spoke, and the meeting was over in half an hour. Alex and Simon were absent since neither sat on the union executive. Following the departure of Drouin and Leduc, sullen faces became animated, and the other members of the executive expressed their opposition to the measures taken against the three of them. While grateful for the support, Nicole left the meeting feeling defeated and powerless.

She stopped off to do some food shopping on the way home. When she entered the apartment, Julie came down the hallway. While Nicole hung up her coat, Julie collected the two bags of groceries and carried them into the kitchen without a word. Nicole walked over to the counter where her daughter was unpacking the food and began to help. Though standing side by side, it felt like they were oceans apart.

Julie finally broke the silence. "How goes the battle?"

"We'll see in a couple of days. There's a membership meeting to vote on another company offer."

"Is it acceptable?"

"Not to me, it isn't, but the guys in the regional office are pushing it. In fact, they've pushed Alex, Simon, and me right off the negotiating committee. They're running the show now."

Julie stopped what she was doing and stared at her mother. "How did that happen?"

Nicole explained the latest developments.

"But the three of you put so much effort into this. And now to be pushed aside, that's not fair."

"Daniel and Claude say we're being unreasonable. But we're just standing our ground like we promised."

Nicole plugged in the kettle, and a sigh escaped. The next thing she knew, there was a hand on her shoulder.

"Take a seat. I'll make some tea," Julie said.

# Chapter 61

There was no doubt in Nicole's mind that those most committed to the struggle opposed their removal from the negotiating committee. But she knew some members welcomed it and suspected others were just relieved to see an end in sight.

In a couple of hours, Leduc and Drouin would be recommending the company's proposal to a mass meeting of the membership. The offer was a convoluted way for management to get the changes it wanted. Alex had called last night and proposed the three of them get together at the union hall, prior to the vote.

He walked into the tiny office and settled on the chair opposite Nicole. The shadows under his eyes suggested she wasn't the only one feeling the strain. Simon arrived shortly after.

"I know people are hurting financially," Alex said, "which means the odds aren't in our favour, but we need to make one last effort at explaining the danger of this proposal." He looked over at Nicole. "As president, you're best placed to do that." When she didn't respond, he turned to Simon. "What are your thoughts on this?"

Simon looked at Alex, then at Nicole. "I agree," he said. "It won't be easy, given the circumstances, but it's our last chance."

Nicole struggled to swallow. Despite their best efforts, here they were, facing the prospect of a demoralizing defeat. How had events reached a point where the regional office was now aligned with management against them? The moisture in her right eye overflowed and trickled down her cheek. She wiped it away and sniffled.

Alex settled back in his chair. "Nicole, do you remember a wee fella who went by the name of Pixie?"

"No."

"He was an old-timer who worked in the machine shop, a real character. I guess he'd retired by the time you arrived. Anyway, the week I started working at Tanner and Ward, he sat down next to me at lunchtime and asked how I'd ended up there. So I told him about the strike at United Aircraft and how some of the lads who led that fight went to jail.

"'They always go after the makers,' he said.

"I asked him what he meant by that.

"'Listen, son,' he said to me, 'I've been here since they opened the doors and seen my share of grabbers who snatch overtime like there's no tomorrow and think that's all that matters in life. Then there's the grumblers who complain about everything and do nothing about anything. And the fakers who talk big but act small. Most of us have behaved this way at one time or other. But we can do better. I know because I've seen it.

"'When this place started up, management ruled like kings. You did what you were told, no questions asked. If you didn't, you weren't around long. This went on for a while. Then some of the lads got together and talked to people after work or went to their homes on weekends. They stuck their necks out, and a few were fired along the way. But because of them, people voted in the union.

"'Those boys were makers,' he said. 'The more we're makers, the less we're grabbers, grumblers, and fakers.'"

Alex paused and leaned forward. "You're a maker, Nicole."

She bowed her head and looked down at her hands. "I don't know how much of a maker I am, Alex. I've made my share of mistakes in life, I know that."

"Makers aren't perfect," he said, "but they're makers all the same."

Rather than looking out on hundreds of members from the dais, Nicole was sitting amongst them when Daniel Leduc opened the meeting. He explained that from now on, he, as business agent, and Claude Drouin, as regional director, would represent the union in all talks with the company. His announcement was met with silence. He passed the microphone to Drouin.

"You've battled this multinational to a standoff," he said. "This offer means you can return to work and receive your regular pay with a three per cent wage increase. Following ratification, the union and management negotiating committees will discuss the issues mentioned in the offer for a period of three months. Whatever cannot be agreed on will be settled by an arbitrator. Simon Arnaud's suspension will be part of that process. The union's lawyer will be working on his case as a top priority.

"We strongly recommend you approve this offer. To do otherwise will only bring more hardship to you and your families with no further gains."

He leaned back in his chair and pushed the microphone over to Leduc, who opened the discussion period.

Steve Fontaine, an assembler who worked with Alex on the T24 line, was first to speak. "If we accept this deal, who's going to be meeting the company to discuss all these issues we haven't reached agreement on?"

"As I explained, Claude and I will represent you in those talks," Leduc replied.

"With all due respect," Fontaine said, "if any of the changes the company wants are implemented, they won't touch either of you. But they will affect the three people you removed from the negotiating committee. That's why we need them in those talks."

Applause broke out.

Drouin wrapped his hand around the microphone and drew it towards him. "Let me assure you brother, Daniel has been part of these negotiations from the beginning, and I've been directly involved for the past few weeks. We know your feelings on these matters and will communicate them to the company. Whatever is agreed to will need to be ratified by you, and everything else will go to an arbitrator."

As Drouin was speaking, Nicole pulled herself up from the chair and made her way to the second microphone. Her legs felt like she had just run up several flights of stairs, and the lump in her throat was so large she could scarcely swallow.

When it was time to recognize the next speaker, Leduc ignored her and signalled towards the other microphone where Tommy Paquette was standing.

Tommy pointed across the room. "Nicole is next."

Drouin grabbed the table microphone. "As Daniel explained at the beginning of this meeting, Nicole Fortin, Alex McCarthy, and Simon Arnaud have been removed from the bargaining committee for challenging the authority of the regional office to lead these talks.

"The purpose of this meeting is not to get into a debate with former members of the negotiating committee but to hear what you, the members, have to say. This is a democratic union, and you will decide its course of action, not a small group of people, either up here, or down there. So in the interest of allowing the members to speak, I would ask Nicole to cede her place to the next person at the microphone."

Some people booed. A few rose from their chairs and gestured toward the front table. From the back of the room, a chant of "let her speak" broke out. Leduc conferred with Drouin as the noise grew louder. Finally, he leaned forward.

"All right, Nicole, the floor is yours."

She ran her tongue back and forth over dry lips, and the floor microphone felt slippery under her touch. "Mr. Chairman, I want to thank our members for their support in this battle with management. The past seven months have proven once again that the only way to protect our rights is to fight for them. That's why the company hasn't achieved its original goals. Now it's changed tactics to try and win through an arbitration process what it hasn't been able to gain so far.

"If those representing us in these discussions continue to defend our rights, as we've done up to now, there will be no agreement on any of the issues the company wants changes on, and they will be referred to an arbitrator. We will be forced to live with his decision and have no further say in the matter. He could side with the company on every single question, in whole or in part.

"I have no problem extending the existing contract while continuing to discuss any outstanding issues the company wants to raise. But I'm against handing over our members' right to choose what kind of agreement we have to work under and giving an arbitrator the power to decide everything.

"We promised to hold the line on any further concessions in these negotiations." Nicole paused and scanned the room. "That's what you've fought for, and so far, we've succeeded. Let's not give in now by agreeing to this deal."

She was interrupted by scattered clapping.

"One more thing. We all know how the grievance system helps management carry on production while people under suspension are left high and dry. Even an expedited case can take many months to be resolved, and in the meantime, the suspended member has no income. We can't go back in and leave Simon outside. The company must withdraw his suspension as part of any settlement. On behalf of Alex, Simon, and myself, I'm asking you to stand firm and vote no."

Pockets of applause erupted across the room.

Leduc pointed to Tommy Paquette at the other microphone. "I move we pass to the vote," he said.

"I second that motion," added a man who was standing behind Nicole.

Leduc pulled the table microphone closer. "Before the voting begins, I want you to understand that if this is rejected, you remain on strike, and there is no guarantee the company will make any further offer in the near future."

It took an hour for the votes to be cast and counted. People were back in their chairs, and there was a buzz of discussion in the hall when Daniel Leduc was handed a piece of paper by the recording secretary. The room fell silent. From where Nicole was sitting, she couldn't see any reaction as he glanced at the paper, before showing it to Drouin. The two men exchanged a few words. Leduc examined the paper in his hands one more time, then leaned toward the microphone. "The offer is rejected by 53.8 per cent."

Alex placed a hand on Nicole's shoulder. "Old Pixie would have been proud."

There was no celebration as people filed out of the hall. Even amongst those who had won the vote, the mood was sombre and the discussion subdued. They resembled a family which had stood watch as a loved one who was terminally ill somehow survived the night. The only question appeared to be how much longer they would be forced to endure the pain until everything was brought to a close.

A snowstorm was creating whiteouts as Nicole drove home from the meeting, reducing traffic to a crawl. Just as she pulled in opposite the apartment, her cell phone rang. She checked the caller ID. "What's up, Alex?"

"Nicole, I just learned Paul Dufour has been released from hospital. I've let Simon know."

"That's good news. I'll call Daniel. If he and Claude are meeting with the company, they should be aware of this."

She dialled Leduc's number. There was no response, so she left a message.

# Chapter 62

Martin Goyette rose from the chair behind his desk and shook hands with Daniel Leduc and Claude Drouin. Moments later, they were joined by Sophie Martel. After a brief exchange, Goyette led them out of the office and down the hallway, where they descended several steps to the basement headquarters of the company's security operation.

Pascal Drolet, supervisor of the guards, walked them through a large room with several monitors connected to cameras trained on various entrances and other strategic points around the property. He gestured towards a smaller room off to the side. A large screen sat at the far end of a rectangular table. Drolet pointed to four chairs, two on each side, and urged everyone to take a seat. Using a keyboard, he entered a password before opening a document identified by a date. He closed the door and dimmed the lights.

"This is the evidence you asked to see," he said. "Copies have been given to the prosecutor's office."

A black and white image of the front entrance appeared on the screen. Picketers could be seen running in the direction of the turnstiles, where they formed a line and locked arms. Suddenly, a phalanx of police appeared, escorting a group of people toward the building. As they approached the turnstiles, a metal fence slid open and the cluster of moving bodies headed for the gap. The picketers rushed towards the police, trying to block their advance. As the two groups collided, several bodies in the centre of the melee went down. Seconds later, Paul Dufour could be seen on his back, lying beside another person. A policeman grabbed the man next to Dufour by his collar and rolled him to the side. It was Simon Arnaud. The screen went blank.

"This is our footage of the incident," Drolet said. "Would you like to see it again?"

Goyette glanced across the table before turning to him. "Please."

After the fourth viewing, he thanked Drolet, who left the room. Half an hour later, Goyette led the other three back to his office.

## Chapter 63

Nicole was sitting behind her desk at the strike headquarters typing on her laptop when the vice-president, Vincent Legault, poked his head through the doorway.

"Hi Vincent, take a seat. I'll be with you in a minute, just answering a member."

"Me too, Nicole, all day long, nothing but questions," he said. "That last meeting shook people up. I had to encourage some of them to get back out there on the picket line."

As he settled into a chair, Nicole stopped typing and looked over at him.

"How's your wife, Vincent?"

He ran a hand across his forehead. "She's just finished a cycle of chemotherapy. Pretty bushed and resting a lot. She has another assessment in three weeks' time. I'd do anything to save her from this, Nicole." He looked back at her with heavy-lidded eyes. "Thirty-nine years we've been married. When we go, it should be together, not separately."

She shifted in her chair. "Look, Vincent, if you need to be at home instead of here, that's okay."

"No," he said. "Her sisters are helping out, and the kids drop by the house. Sometimes it's better to be elsewhere. At least I can put my anger to use here."

Nicole's cell phone rang. He rose to leave, but she motioned for him to stay.

"This is Daniel. We just heard from Goyette. There will be a meeting at nine o'clock Wednesday morning to vote on a new company proposal at the Crowne Plaza. Please make sure the members are informed."

He declined to give any further details and said Drouin was still verifying one aspect of the offer. After the call ended, Nicole turned to Legault.

"That was Daniel Leduc. The company's made another offer. We need to activate the phone tree. There's a meeting Wednesday morning."

"What's the offer?"

"He wouldn't give me any information and said they were still checking something. I guess we'll find out at the meeting."

"I don't like that," Legault said. "We should have a chance to see what we're voting on before then."

"I agree, but Daniel and Claude are running the show now."

# Chapter 64

Nicole was seated next to Simon and Alex in the middle of the crowd when Daniel Leduc lifted the walnut gavel and banged it three times against the round wooden block sitting on the table in front of him. The hum of conversation dried up, and people turned in his direction. Along with Claude Drouin, he was seated on the dais behind a table covered by a white cloth. A pitcher of water, two glasses, and a table microphone sat before them.

"Will the stewards please close the doors?" he said. "We're ready to begin.

"Following a meeting on Monday with company representatives, we received a new offer from management. Claude will explain it."

Leduc passed the microphone to Drouin.

"Good morning, brothers and sisters. The company is proposing to extend the existing collective agreement for fifteen months with a three per cent wage increase to cover that period. This is what you voted on before. However, there are two changes.

"Along with Martin Goyette and Sophie Martel, we reviewed the taped evidence of the incident that led to the injury of Paul Dufour. Based on what we saw, the company decided to rescind its suspension of Simon Arnaud and asked the prosecution to withdraw the charges against him. We've just received word that request has been accepted. The case has been dropped."

Simon closed his eyes and clenched his hands into fists. Nicole grasped him by the forearm, and Alex squeezed his shoulder. The room broke into applause and whistles. Drouin waited for the noise to subside.

"As we explained last time, the company has proposed that four questions be referred to the union and management negotiating committees for further discussion over the next three months. Anything agreed to will have to be ratified by you. What cannot be resolved will be referred to an arbitrator. But here, there's a second change. Although his recommendations will be taken into account by both parties in future negotiations, they will not be binding. I think that removes any reason for not accepting this proposal, and we're recommending it to you."

Drouin passed the microphone back to Leduc.

"Is there any discussion before the vote?"

Annie leapt up to one of the floor microphones.

Leduc nodded at her. "Go ahead."

"If this proposal is accepted, management won't be able to use an arbitrator to impose the changes it wants. But there's still one other issue to sort out here," she said. "We need the three elected members of our negotiating committee in those discussions with the company. They live what we live on the shop floor, and if they're not part of those talks, then we aren't either."

Applause broke out. Some people rose to their feet and shouted, "Take them back!"

Leduc leaned over to Drouin, and they exchanged a few words as the clamour grew louder. Finally, Leduc raised his hands and asked for silence. He passed the microphone to Drouin.

"If the offer is accepted today, the trusteeship of this local will be lifted, and the negotiating committee will consist of Daniel, myself, and the three members elected by you. The five of us will participate in discussions with management on the unresolved issues in dispute."

People stood and cheered. Annie looked back at Nicole with a huge grin and gave her the thumbs up.

"Is there any more discussion?" Leduc shouted over the noise. "Those in favour of moving to the vote, raise your hands. Those opposed."

People were already scrambling for the hallway where the booths were set up. Drouin and Leduc remained in their chairs as the mass of bodies snaked by below them. Fifteen minutes later, people were filing in after casting their ballot, while others were still edging their way out of the room toward the booths.

The atmosphere had been transformed from one of nervous tension to celebration. Once the voting was completed and the ballots counted, Leduc was handed the results. He announced the offer had been approved by 95.3 per cent, and the room exploded in applause and cheers one last time.

After the meeting broke up, the hotel bar was packed, and people overflowed into the surrounding hallway. Requests by staff to keep drinks within the confines of the bar went unheeded, and they soon gave up the effort, buoyed along by the good cheer that flowed through the crowd.

Everyone knew they had only set a new date for the next battle in twelve months' time. But at least for now, they celebrated their victory.

# Chapter 65

At a meeting between the union and company negotiating committees two weeks into the three-month discussion period, Martin Goyette announced that he would be leaving to head up Tanner and Ward's operation in Dallas, Texas, effective immediately.

Charles Allard, the director of Human Resources, was to lead the company's negotiating team in the meantime. Goyette's successor was expected to be named within the week. Meanwhile, both sides were just rehashing the same arguments.

On her drive home from the meeting, Nicole was caught in bumper-to-bumper traffic and found herself reflecting on Goyette's announcement. She hadn't been able to tell from his reaction whether he was excited by the move or merely pleased to be rid of them. As she was mulling this over, a driver two cars ahead attempted to change lanes and squeeze into a space that wasn't there. Screeching tires provoked a chorus of honking horns, and Nicole was forced to concentrate on the reality of rush-hour traffic.

Upon reaching the apartment, she checked the mailbox and found a letter whose return address was for a law firm on the West Island. She had no dealings with anyone out that way and wondered if it had something to do with the injunctions or the strike.

After exchanging her boots for slippers, she hung up her coat, dropped the letter on the kitchen table, and filled the kettle.

While the water boiled, she took a knife from the drawer and opened the envelope. Three pages were folded over. The top one explained that Gabriel Nadeau had requested the enclosed information be sent to Nicole Fortin on his death.

She reached out for the kitchen table to steady herself and sank onto a chair. The second page was addressed to her and signed by Gabriel. "Although I cannot undo what happened between us," he wrote, "now that events have reached this stage for me, I think the enclosed information should be passed on to you."

Nicole slid the second sheet under the other two and stared at the third page. It had the name and address of a clinic at the top. She read the page a second time to be sure she understood. The water hissed, and she unplugged the kettle. Seconds later, the front door opened, and Julie called out a greeting.

Nicole removed two mugs from the cupboard and set them on the table next to the sheets of paper. Her daughter had lost a father she would never meet.

# Chapter 66

Alex walked into the union office as Nicole was working her way through the daily backlog of emails. "You asked to see me?"

"Yeah. Simon can't join us because he took a personal day to look at a larger apartment. Just let me finish answering this."

"No problem," he said and sank into a chair.

A minute later, she clicked send and turned off the computer.

Alex rubbed a hand across the back of his neck. "How is Julie these days?"

"Immersed in school assignments from what I gather."

He nodded. "She's a bright one. She'll pull through."

Nicole gestured at the papers strewn across her desk, "I'm just keeping my own head above water."

"I'd expect nothing less," Alex said. "After all, you are a swimmer."

His comment produced a slight grin before she became serious again. "I just received some information on Jeremy Benson. It's not good news."

Alex swung one leg over the other. "Why am I not surprised by that?"

Martin Goyette's successor had been named the previous week. Nicole had reached out to the union representing Tanner and Ward's employees in the UK to see what she could find out about the man.

"Apparently Benson's a rising star in upper management. He's currently vice-president at one of their manufacturing plants in Britain. But prior to that, he was sent to Brazil with a mandate to shut down a facility that was 'underperforming.' Three hundred people lost their jobs. His assignment to Montreal is seen as a step up the ladder."

Alex stroked his chin. "So Goyette was the sheep in wolf's clothing, and now they're sending out the genuine article."

"Looks that way."

He sank back in his chair and ran a hand through his hair. "People like this Benson character come here for a couple of years, do their damage, and leave destruction in their wake." He paused and then sighed. "I don't know how many more of these fights I can take part in, Nicole. I'm starting to feel my age."

Something caught in her throat. She couldn't imagine him not being by her side.

"You look fit enough to me, Alex."

He stared at the floor and said nothing.

Nicole gnawed at the inside of her cheek.

Finally, he looked up. "Aye, maybe I'm good for one more round."

He pushed himself up from the chair and took a step towards the door. Then he stopped and turned back to her. "We may not win every battle. But at least we're on the right side of history."

Nicole smiled at him. "And who could ask for more than that."

# Acknowledgements

The path to this book began with the discovery of the Quebec Writers' Federation and its twice-yearly writing workshops.

Books are always associated with the names of their authors, which gives the mistaken impression that they are simply the result of individual effort. Nothing could be further from the truth.

My thanks to Michael Cadogan, Licia Canton, Maya Merrick, Elise Moser, Dimitri Nasrallah, Ian Thomas Shaw, Cora Siré, and Jack Todd, who provided valuable feedback on various drafts. None of them are responsible for whatever errors or weaknesses remain. Also to Michael Cohen, Angelo Falbo, Peter McCambridge, Rachel McCrum, and Danny Morrison for their assistance.

Thanks to Blossom Thom and Rachel Hewitt for their editorial and proofreading work and to the team at Maison 1608 for the cover design.

I am most indebted to Robin Philpot, President and Publisher of Baraka Books. Without his interest and effort, this book would not exist.

**Notable fiction from Baraka Books**

*Exile Blues* by Douglas Gary Freeman
*Things Worth Burying* by Matt Mayr
*Fog* by Rana Bose
*The Daughters' Story* by Murielle Cyr
*Yasmeen Haddad Loves Joanasi Maqaittik*
by Carolyn Marie Souaid
The Nickel Range Trilogy by Mick Lowe
*The Raids*
*The Insatiable Maw*
*Wintersong*

Novels from QC Fiction, an imprint of Baraka Books

*Songs for the Cold of Heart* by Eric Dupont
(translated by Peter McCambridge)
*Life in the Court of Matane* by Eric Dupont
(translated by Peter McCambridge)
*The Woman in Valencia* by Annie Perreault
(translated by Ann Marie Boulanger)

Nonfiction

*Stolen Motherhood, Surrogacy and Made-to-Order Children*
Maria De Koninck
*Still Crying for Help, The Failure of Our Mental Healthcare Services*
Sadia Messaili
*A Distinct Alien Race, The Untold Story of Franco-Americans*
David Vermette
*The Einstein File, The FBI's Secret War
on the World's Most Famous Scientist*
Fred Jerome
*Through the Mill
Girls and Women in the Quebec Cotton Textile Industry 1881-1951*
Gail Cuthbert Brandt

Printed by Imprimerie Gauvin
Gatineau, Québec